Chills Run Down My Spine

When Mickey finds himself abandoned in a
terrifying haunted house, he discovers more than
ghosts and learns that nothing is stranger than human
nature: "Haunted houses can send chills down your
spine, but there's nothing – in life or after –
half as cold as hate."

In this, the title story, and the other eight stories in
this chilling collection, Jackie Vivelo gives traditional
ghost stories a subtle twist as she explores deeper and
darker secrets and emotions. Who is the strange dog
that saves Jared from a pack of wild dogs, and why
can't Grandfather see it? Can Hope's cousin Boyd
really be a murderer – just by wishing? Who or what
can be so frightening that it sends Sara's mean
Uncle Ted running out of the house in sheer terror?
And why does Janet's new friend Meg never come to
her house and refuse to meet her family? Is she shy,
or is there another, stranger reason?

Certain to send delicious trickles of icy fear down
your spine, these are stories to share by reading aloud,
or to read on your own ... if you dare.

JACKIE
VIVELO

Chills

Run

Down

My

Spine

A DORLING KINDERSLEY BOOK

To Alexandra

First published in Great Britain in 1994
by Dorling Kindersley Limited,
9 Henrietta Street, London WC2E 8PS

A CIP catalogue record for this book is
available from the British Library

ISBN 0-7513-7028-2

Printed and bound in Great Britain by
Butler & Tanner Ltd, Frome and London

Illustrated by Jennifer Eachus
Designed by Ian Butterworth

CONTENTS

Time

is

but

the

stream

I

go

a-fishing

in.

HENRY DAVID THOREAU

"**L**ook!" Mrs Hillman exclaimed. "I think she must be about your age, Mo."

Both Maureen and her younger sister Janet craned to see out of the window as the car sped past the girl standing on the bottom rail of a wooden fence.

"She looks like she could be **my** age," Janet said.

"No, she's my age," Maureen said.

"Of course she is," Mrs Hillman agreed with her elder daughter. "It will be wonderful to have someone for you to spend time with."

Janet made one more brief protest, was overridden, and gave up. She had trouble understanding why a companion was so much more important for her elder sister. Didn't she count at all? Didn't anybody care whether she found a friend for the next three months?

The car turned into the long drive leading to the farmhouse where they'd come to stay for the summer. By

looking out of the back window, Janet could still see the
girl on the fence. That must mean she was a neighbour.
Well, she could wait to find out the girl's age, but she
was sure she had as much chance of being right as Mom
and Mo, as they always called Maureen.

Half an hour later, Mo was in the bathroom plaiting
her hair. Janet, unpacking her things, heard her mother
telling her father, "Thank goodness there's another
teenager in the area. She should help keep Maureen
busy. Janet, of course, will take care of herself."

Janet felt a rush of anger. At nine, she had different
interests from her thirteen-year-old sister, but surely her
parents ought to know they'd **both** like friends. For
three months she'd be stuck here in the woods.

During the afternoon, Mrs Hillman spotted the same
girl walking across a field and told her daughters, both of
them, to go and introduce themselves.

"Hi," the girl called out when they were close enough
to hear. She gave them a big grin and hurried to meet
them. "I was hoping there would be kids this year."

"Hi, I'm Maureen – call me Mo – and this is my
sister Janet."

"I'm Carolyn Gillespie."

The three girls sat on a large stone and talked. Carolyn
was a non-stop talker.

She told them how one summer when she was very
young, Brady Fields, the famous teen model and actress,
had stayed in that same old farmhouse for a week.

"She had a grazed knee just like anybody else might

have. But I barely got to see her, and she was older than I was anyway. I was just a little kid then. So how old are you two?"

After Janet said she was nine and Mo said she was thirteen, Carolyn told them she was eleven, which gave Janet a lot of satisfaction. She had been right, as right as her mother and Mo had been. But the satisfaction was all she got. Before they split up to go home, Mo made plans to meet Carolyn the next morning, plans that didn't include Janet.

Because her father had taken the farmhouse as a retreat in which to finish his book on Alfred the Great, both girls were supposed to be out of the house by nine o'clock or, if they were still inside, to be absolutely quiet.

The first week Mo and Carolyn spent every day together. Sometimes they both brought picnic lunches and ate in the field; sometimes they ate at Carolyn's house. And on some days, Carolyn's mother took them to the swimming pool in the nearby town. With each passing day, Janet felt lonelier. Her mother had said she should give the other two some time together. But Janet had made up her mind to beg, if necessary, to be allowed to join them. She was kneeling beside the stream that ran through the farm property when she decided she wouldn't spend another day on her own. Sure, the woods were great, but she wanted someone to talk to.

In the sunlight filtering through the tree branches on her side of the stream, she saw minnows in the clear depths of the water. Quickly she became intent on catching one in her bare hands. The minnow got away, but her eye was attracted to a whole line of tiny fish that, one at a time, swam behind a rock at the far side of the water. Pulling off her shoes and sticking one under each arm, she waded into the shallow water for a better look.

"Look how they dart into that shadow behind the rock and they don't come out again." She had spoken out loud as she often did when she was alone.

"They have to come out. If they didn't, there'd be a whole pile of them back there."

Janet saw the girl's reflection in the water before she looked up to see a redhead about her own age kneeling on the other side of the shallow stream.

Cautiously, Janet moved forwards in the water, trying not to scare the fish. The ones around her feet swam off swiftly, but those headed for the rock still stayed in a sort of line.

"They aren't coming out," she repeated. "They have to be going somewhere that we can't see."

"I'm going to look from this side," the other girl said. "If we have to, we can dig up the rock."

United in a common interest, the two girls took each other's cooperation for granted.

"I'm coming with you," Janet said, climbing out on the other girl's side.

"I think we have to push these grasses aside."

"Ayeek!" Janet cried, almost falling back into the water.

"What is it? What's wrong?"

Janet looked up from the water and directly at the girl beside her, who looked back with concern.

"There's a snake there. See the black line beyond the rock?"

"So? I'm not scared of snakes."

"It's eating the fish. It's swallowing every one that swims into the shadow."

Side by side, the girls watched. Each time a fish swam round the rock, the snake – in a slow, casual movement – ate it.

"You wouldn't think they'd all line up just to get eaten," Janet said, pointing at all the fish still headed that way.

"I guess they don't know. None of the fish have come back to warn them."

That was how Janet met Meg. The hidden snake was an odd sort of thing to have watched, and it gave Janet the feeling the two of them had already been friends for a long time.

"Are there other kids our age around here?" Janet asked.

Meg shook her head.

"Who do you play with when I'm not here?"

"My cat. I always have my cat and her kittens."

The rest of the day was so filled with activities that Janet soon forgot the cat and kittens. First they cut reeds by the stream and made them into whistles. Then they spent all afternoon learning to play them.

By the end of the day, in addition to Meg's name, Janet had learned that she was also nine years old, that she lived "over there", and that she wanted to meet Janet by the stream the next morning.

"Look at the apple tree," Meg said. "It's still early enough to grow an apple in a bottle. Could you bring us two tomorrow?"

"What kind of bottles?"

"You need the kind with skinny necks but big and round at the bottom. Then when the apple gets ripe, it's like magic, too big to go through the bottle's neck."

When Janet got home that second day, she tried the rubbish bin and then poked around among the old junk in the cellar and finally found two good bottles. One was an economy-sized ketchup bottle with a long, thin neck and a big base. The other was an old green wine bottle with a narrow neck and a rounded bottom like a balloon. She put them under the back steps until the next morning.

Meg and Janet went straight to the old apple tree first thing and slipped the bottles over the little nubs that would grow into apples, resting the bottles against the branches and taping them in place.

Now Janet too had a reason to pack a lunch because she and Meg spent all of each day together. Finding a trail of ants, the two girls placed bigger and bigger crumbs in their path, amazed at the ability of the tiny creatures to carry away bits of bread and cheese many times their own size.

They found a wasps' nest and a hornets' nest, saw honeycomb made by bees, and lay by the water to watch the dragonflies' gauze-like wings shimmer in the sun. After examining the clay home of the dauber wasps, they made an imitation one on the riverbank. They climbed a tree for a closer look at the huge papery shell that housed the hornets but slid down again, scraping their legs on the bark in their rush to get away when they attracted the hornets' attention. They spent hours studying a dragonfly as it walked on the water's surface, then took to the air, and finally captured a fly by curling its legs round it like a basket.

"What do you do all day?" Mrs Hillman asked when Janet turned down a long-delayed chance to go on a trip with Carolyn and her parents.

"I'm spending time with Meg. We just do things."

"I'm getting worried about you. Why don't you go out for the day with Mo and Carolyn instead of that imaginary playmate?"

So they thought Meg wasn't real! Janet was too angry to speak. If Meg wasn't real, how had Janet learned to gather spruce gum, which was great for chewing? How did she know that you find monarch butterfly cocoons on milkweed? How had she managed to plant a willow shoot and get it to grow? She hadn't known about any of those things before Meg showed her.

In disgust, Janet wandered back outdoors after supper, wishing Meg had told her just where she lived. They always met each morning by the stream and said

good-bye on the bank of the stream each afternoon. Meg
was not only real, she was the best friend Janet had
ever had.

The next day Janet asked Meg if she would go along
on the Gillespies' trip, but Meg just shook her head.

"Please come," Janet said, not wanting to tell Meg that
no one believed she really existed.

Meg didn't look up from the grasses she was weaving
into a mat. She just shook her head again.

"Why not? Why won't you go?"

"The cats," Meg answered.

And nothing Janet said could persuade her friend to
say more.

The two girls continued each day to check first on
their apples that were growing to fill the bottles and then
on their rapidly growing willow shoots.

They trailed butterflies in the field, made wishes by
blowing the seeds of dandelions, and found dozens of
"secret" birds' nests, including a family of owls in a
split oak.

Lying on the bank of the stream one day late in the
summer, Janet watched sunlight dance on the rushing
water. She thought of all the things she'd seen for the
first time that summer: black bugs that curled into a ball
when she dropped them into her palm and leaves that
closed up when she stroked them, wild berries she could
safely pick and eat and wild blue flowers that wilted the
minute they were picked, birds that imitated any sound
they heard, and frogs that lived in trees. Despite all they

had already done, each day Meg had something new to do or show.

Janet rolled on to one elbow and looked at Meg's curly red hair; glints of gold made it seem as if the sun danced on it too.

"I don't think I'd ever get tired of this."

Meg turned her face with its wide cheeks towards Janet and grinned. "Me, neither."

"So, if she's real, bring her with you," Mo argued.

Summer was almost over and in a few days the Hillmans would go back to the university town where Mr Hillman taught.

"It's your last chance to go to a swimming party. I'm putting my foot down about this," Mrs Hillman said. "The Gillespies have invited you too, and I want you to go with them on Saturday."

"I guess I have to say good-bye," Janet told Meg the following afternoon. "We're leaving day after tomorrow, and I have to spend tomorrow with my sister and her friend. Couldn't I come and say good-bye to you early on Sunday morning before we leave? Where's your house?"

Meg shook her head. Then as an afterthought, she added, "I wouldn't be there anyway. I'd be in the barn."

"Why?"

"Because that's where my cats are."

Janet made a face and then gave up. She didn't understand, but she could see Meg didn't want her to come and say good-bye. And maybe that was better. In a way, she'd always have this summer. She knew she would never forget it or Meg.

That afternoon they picked their bottled apples. The apple, too big to come out of the bottle, was something real to show her family. Meg made Janet take the one in the green wine bottle because the other one had grown lopsided in the ketchup bottle.

Before they said good-bye for the last time beside the stream, Janet said, "This was the best summer of my life. I'm glad I came here."

"Me too," Meg said.

The next day was better than Janet had expected it to be. Carolyn's father and mother, together with Carolyn, Mo, Janet, and two other girls rode in the Gillespies' estate car to a state park where there were picnic areas and a lake for swimming. Even though she got sunburned, Janet enjoyed the day.

On the way home she sat beside Mrs Gillespie, who – like her daughter – kept up a constant stream of talk. After a day in the sun, the motion of the car and the soft, steady voice recounting stories about the area soon had Janet nodding off to sleep. The first time she was startled awake was when her head fell forwards. The second time, through her half-dream, she heard Meg's name and immediately snapped to attention.

"Did you ever meet her?" Janet asked Mrs Gillespie.

"Oh, yes, of course."

"Will we pass her house?" Janet asked. "Could you

show me?"

"Didn't you know?" Mrs Gillespie asked, surprised.

"She used to live in the same house you're staying in."

"But **now**? I mean, where does she live now?"

Mrs Gillespie looked at her strangely.

"You see, there was a barn just on the other side of the stream, and one day it caught fire. Oh, it was a long time ago; you needn't look so worried. They weren't able to save it. It burned right to the ground, but before it was gone, in the worst heat of the blaze, Meg went running into it. No one could get in to her, and she never came out."

For Carolyn's mother this was just one more story to tell, but Janet felt a freezing coldness in her throat.

"But why?" She swallowed hard and something like ice travelled all the way down and settled in her stomach. "Why would she go into a burning barn?"

"She had a cat," Mrs Gillespie said, "and the cat had kittens there in the barn. Meg went back to save them."

I

wasn't

born

in

a

wood

to

be

scared

by

an

owl.

BELLE'S STRATAGEM, 1780

Mrs Hannah Cowley

CRADLE
SONG

Ben had come to live with us when his own family was killed in a fire. Father, mother, uncle, sisters – all were gone at once, and only Ben survived. Until he came I'd been an only child, so you might think I'd have been jealous, but I was never anything but glad – glad for his company, glad for someone to share the blame for the trouble we got into, glad for new ideas of things to do.

Ben had lots of new ideas. His own family had been so different from ours, more noisy, more rough-and-tumble. I thought at first Ben and I would always be in trouble for the things we did together. But my mother never minded.

"Don't hurt each other," she would say. Over and over she'd remind me, "Ben's different; just respect his ways. Respect him and he'll respect you."

Watching us together, my dad would grin and say,

"Those two are **good** for each other. Ben's the best thing that has happened to this family."

You would think we would have been good for Ben, and I guess we were. We took him in when he had no one else. And we really did make him one of our family, but there were times when I could see nothing would ever make up for what he had lost.

The truth is Ben was haunted. It wasn't the family he lost in the fire. Maybe a ghost or two of that kind would have been easier to understand. No, Ben was haunted by a song.

The two of us were lying on our stomachs looking into the fireplace. Above the crackle of the wood, the sound of popcorn popping drowned out the wind whistling in the chimney, at least for the moment. With a last burst of sound the popcorn finished, and the wind came back with its eerie cry. I pushed myself up to go for the popcorn, and Ben began his tuneless, wordless song.

"What does it mean, Mom?" I asked. I had heard it several times before, always when Ben seemed distracted, lost in thought. I think I knew he wasn't with us when he was singing it, and I resented his absence.

"Ssh!" Mom said, drawing me towards the stove and away from Ben and the hearth. "It's his heritage, his past. It's like a lullaby you only half remember, but you belong to your heritage."

Even though that sounded strange to me, I only answered, "It doesn't sound like any lullaby I ever heard."

"Cradle songs stay with us, even if we don't remember them right or remember them fully, or even remember them at all. Ben had another family; he lost them all; he lost a way of life. Don't be jealous of his past."

I could see tears shining in her eyes, as I took the popcorn from her. Thoughtfully, I carried it back to the hearth.

Later that evening I caught a scrap of a conversation between my parents. I overheard my dad say, "It's strange that Ben doesn't mind the fire. Did you see the two of them settled down on the hearth?"

Sometimes in the night Ben would wake me with that almost tuneless but always recognizable song. I'd remind myself of the fire that killed his family and tell myself that it was his cradle song. I was glad I had never complained to Ben.

Ben was younger than I, but he grew faster and to my chagrin he grew stronger and more muscular. He seemed to know, without anyone teaching him, how to track animals through the woods. When the two of us were out together, he'd just naturally take the lead. Several times he took us right up to a clearing where deer were. The nearest view I'd ever had of deer came on one of our expeditions when I followed Ben to the lake beyond Kuyper's Hill.

We were walking along when he suddenly froze and stared intently ahead.

"What is it?" I asked. "What do you see?" By this time I knew enough to whisper. Ben never stopped like that without a reason.

I almost had to push him aside to get a look, but when I did, I could see why the scene fascinated him. Just beyond a screen of leaves stood a doe with two fawns. Swimming out a few metres from the shore was the biggest stag I'd ever seen. His antlers looked like the branches of a sunken tree.

Ben had found them. He always seemed at home in the woods, and I was willing to follow his lead.

Wherever we went, he found adventure. Not only had I been without brothers or sisters before Ben came along, but because we lived in such an isolated spot, I had had few playmates.

I never thought about the difference in our ages. I never felt superior. (Well, the truth is, I wasn't – not in size or strength or knowledge of the world.) I guess I'm trying to say I never did anything to make Ben want to leave. I wanted him to stay with us forever.

Spring, summer, autumn were all good seasons with Ben. We never lacked things to do. We'd race; Ben would win, of course, though I could see he was sometimes tempted to let me beat him. I could see him look back and consider slowing down so I could pass him or maybe just catch up. He never did. I think he knew I had too much pride to win that way. We also fished together, and I was a little better at that than Ben was.

We explored without fear of getting lost because Ben's sense of direction never failed. Maybe his ancestors had travelled across continents guiding themselves by the sun and stars. If that kind of thing is hereditary, my ancestors must have spent all their lives in the same place. I can get lost only a hundred metres from home.

One spring night I heard Ben stir in his bed against the opposite wall from mine. Without raising my head or speaking, I opened my eyes and watched as he got up and padded silently to the window, where he stood staring out.

The moon was full and so bright it lit the room with a soft glow. I slipped out of bed and stood beside him by the window.

"Do you think we could go out?" I suggested. "It looks as bright as day."

We live on the edge of a forest that stretches to the mountains. I had never been encouraged to go outside at night. On the other hand I'd never wanted to before, so no one had actually said it was forbidden.

I had to search under the bed for my shoes, but with as little fuss as possible, Ben and I slipped downstairs and out of the house.

Once outside, Ben began to run. Stumbling at first, I hurled myself after him. We ran, leaping over fallen branches, scuffling through troughs still filled with the dead leaves of winter, even jumping a small creek. Never before had I experienced anything like that wild night run. We stopped on a ridge just where the foothills began, still miles from the mountains.

My blood had been pounding so loud in my ears that I hadn't heard anything else. Now side by side, catching our breath on the slope, we stood and listened to a distant sound. It made my skin prickle.

"What –" I began. But I didn't need to ask. On a far slope, across the lake that lay at the foot of our ridge, I could see black shapes dotting the hillside. I knew without asking that they were wolves.

The sight made me cold in a way the night air hadn't done. Maybe **I** was afraid of the wilderness, but not Ben. Day or night, deer or wolves, he wasn't afraid. Something about that sound reminded me that I was the older one here, the one who was supposed to be responsible, no matter how much I usually relied on Ben. I clapped a hand on his shoulder.

"Let's go home," I urged.

I almost had to tug him away. He seemed hypnotized by what we'd found. Well, what **he'd** found. He was a natural woodsman. But he tore his eyes away and reluctantly turned towards home. We set a slower pace this time.

Lying in bed in the hours after midnight, I remembered the wolf pack baying at the moon and I was glad I had Ben to share my bedroom, not that I talked about what we had seen, but I heard him stirring restlessly until I fell asleep.

Summer was the best of all with Ben. For most of my

life I had been on my own in the summer. Now I had a companion.

One day we were lying by a stream, not fishing, just cooling off in some deep green grasses under the trees by the water's edge. I was pulling the long blades of grass and chewing on the tender ends. I think I must have been half asleep by the time I heard the splashing.

I opened my eyes and sat up to see Ben churning up mud, half walking, half treading water out into the stream. A mother duck from somewhere upstream had come sailing along with her nearly grown ducklings, and Ben was going after them.

"You idiot!" I yelled.

Ben ignored me.

"Leave them alone!" I threw away the long piece of grass I was still holding and got to my feet. Barefoot, barelegged, I plunged into the stream, but Ben had already caught a duckling. The mother and the rest of her brood had climbed out on the far side from us, where they were quacking away like crazy.

Ben turned back towards our bank and we reached it at about the same time. Gently he put the duckling on the matted grass there. It looked dazed, half-dead from fright maybe, but otherwise okay. Nothing was broken, and it could stand up.

"Can we put it back?" I asked. "What'd you want to go and do that for?"

But I knew the answer. Everything in nature interested him, seemed to be a part of him. He hadn't, after all, hurt the duckling. He had just wanted to see it.

We put it back in the stream and it paddled frantically towards the others who slid into the water to meet it and paddle on. Only the mother looked back to direct a few more comments at Ben.

From time to time, I'd still hear Ben singing. Any time he thought no one was around, he might launch into his song. At those times I seemed to feel his loneliness, and it made me lonely too – and angry. Why should he feel lonely when he had me?

Late in the autumn I had a party and invited some friends from my class at school. Two days before the party an early snowfall blanketed the hills. The roads were clear by the day of the party, but the snow was still deep enough for some sledding and skiing. Ben stayed home, partly because he didn't know these guys and partly because he wasn't interested in sledding and skiing.

We spent all afternoon in the snow, then grilled hamburgers for supper. The others had left when Tony, a friend who was going to stay overnight, suggested we put on the cross-country skis and go out once more. We were moving along at a good pace, and I was trying to keep Tony in sight, when I realized that darkness was coming faster than we had counted on.

"Let's start back," I called.

Tony didn't hear or decided to push on a little farther anyway. We went on over the crest of a pine-covered

rise. Doggedly, I followed. I couldn't turn back
without him.

When I caught up with him, I said, "Tony, we have to
go back. These hills are tricky in the dark. Besides," I
admitted, "it's easy to get lost."

We turned, went up the hill we'd just come down, and
were heading down the slope on the other side when I
realized I was already lost. I might have got us back in
the light but not in the darkening twilight.

"Don't worry. I'll get us back," Tony said when I
told him.

Moments later I heard a crash and knew from the
sounds that Tony had hit a tree.

I called his name, peered uselessly around in the
fading light, and then set off in the general direction of
that thud. Right away I was in trouble myself. I went
over a boulder, easy to avoid in daylight but now
invisible, and slid into a snowbank.

I'd hardly begun to pull myself out when I felt the
snow being scooped away. My head emerged, and I was
just about to say, "Thanks, Tony," when I realized it
wasn't Tony. The face looking into mine was Ben's. He
had been following us on that run.

He might not care for snow sports, but he knew those
woods. He led the way to Tony, who was winded and
speechlessly thankful for the rescue.

Tony and I had gone farther than we meant to, and on
the trip back we both had time to realize we probably
owed our lives to Ben.

You don't grow up in the woods without learning a
thing or two about staying alive. But that winter Ben
taught me more about courage and about the woods that
were my home. It wasn't that Ben was courageous; he
was fearless, and that's a different thing. He had no fear
of the forest, the animals, the weather. I'm not saying
that was smart, but it's the way he was. On the other
hand, I was afraid of a lot of things, even though I
stayed with Ben on all his explorations, but I most
needed courage for what happened that next spring.

Christmas came and went and the worst of the snows
were past. One moonlit night in mid-March, Ben and I
were out for another night run.

Just as it had been on that first run almost a year
earlier, the moon was full but brighter than ever against
the icy crust of leftover snow. As we ran, we sometimes
broke through the crust. It wasn't an easy run or a
smooth one. As though he'd known just where to go,
Ben led us out of a stand of fir trees to a clearing.

And there they were, the little group of wolves, only
this time they were much closer to us. At first we stood
and watched as we had before. I think I knew what was
going to happen as soon as I saw them, but maybe I just
tell myself that now. This part I do know for sure: Ben
looked at me and he said good-bye. In his own way, he
said good-bye.

I understood without any words. I saw what he was
going to do, and I knew nothing I could say would stop

him. He set off at an easy lope as though all the distance we had covered hadn't meant anything.

By the light of the moon I watched him join the wolves, lift his face to the sky, and give voice to his song. I'd heard it a lot over the past two years but never like this.

On our hearth or in the garden, even on the hill above the creek, Ben's song had been sad, an echo from some other place. For the first time it was right, as right as the night, as the stars. That song was beautiful.

My throat felt too tight for me to breathe; I knew we had lost him. Ben had found the ones who shared his song. Not the family he had lost in the forest fire, but a family he would belong to as he couldn't belong to mine.

The air was clear and biting cold under a navy blue sky. I could see Ben and the wolf pack plainly against the snow, and I looked hard to memorize his shape among the others, proud head with muzzle lifted to the sky and ears laid back along the dark fur of his neck. It took all of my courage to say good-bye to my brother – to Ben, my brother the wolf.

"The burned area is growing well," my father said. "Of course, the birds were back last spring, but this year other animals are moving in as well."

I was lying on my stomach in front of the fire, only half listening to the voices behind me.

"I suppose," my mother said after a pause, "Ben

had to go."

My father didn't speak right away and I lay listening to the crackle of the flames.

"The wolf pack is growing larger," he said at last. "By next year Ben may be back at the same den where his family once lived, back to start a family of his own."

They went on speaking, but instead of their voices I heard again the strange, deep-throated song that Ben had sung until it finally drew him away from us, and I closed my eyes imagining his great, furry body stretched beside me on the hearth.

One

good

turn

deserves

another.

FOLK SAYING

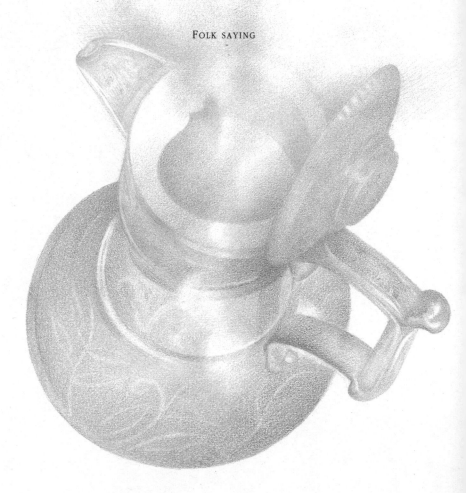

At first it had only been Miss Fisher's
Uncle Ted. Uncle Ted was much too young to retire but
he had a bad back.

"You have that great big house and no one to take
care of. You might as well take care of me," Uncle Ted
had said.

Sara Fisher had been quite happy in her big house
taking care of herself and Scotty, her dog. She intended
to tell Uncle Ted he couldn't move in; but, while she was
trying to think of a nice way to say no, he kept rumbling
on about how bad his "lumbargo" was and saying that
what he needed was a big, sunny room just like the
corner one upstairs with its own little balcony.

Naturally, the corner room with the balcony was Sara's
bedroom, but before she knew what was happening she
found all her things moved to the next largest bedroom
and Uncle Ted moved in, snug and pleased with himself.

With Sara's house to live in and Sara to cook and clean for him, Uncle Ted gave up his job and began spending all day playing draughts, sometimes on the courthouse steps, other times in a nearby tavern.

"It all comes," Sara told Scotty, "of being too slow to think of ways to say no, because it's a fact that you and I didn't need him here."

"Has your father come to live with you?" asked Karen, the little girl from next door, when she and her brother Edward came over to borrow sugar.

"No, that's my Uncle Ted."

Sara didn't complain, but Karen and Edward could see that she looked sadder than she used to.

They had always liked to watch her hang clothes on the line, an activity that interested them because their mother put clothes in a machine to dry. In the time before Uncle Ted came, Sara Fisher used to do a sort of dance, moving down the line as she changed a night-gown partner for a sleeveless dress. She still looked neat and pretty in her blue and white dress, but she didn't dance down the clothes-line any more.

Watching her, Karen and Edward frowned. But for the moment, they couldn't think of anything to do about the change in their nice neighbour.

Then one day without warning, Sara Fisher's life went from not-as-good-as-usual to just-about-awful. It happened when Uncle Ted told her he had invited his daughter Vera and her husband Leon to live with them.

Sara was speechless.

"It isn't forever. They just need a place to live until they can find an apartment in the city. And you do have all this space."

Once Sara had had "all this space". Now Sara had three large people living in her house, expecting her to feed them, wash their clothes, and run their errands. It quickly began to look as though they were all there to stay. Vera and Leon only looked at one apartment and decided it wasn't nearly as nice as Sara Fisher's house. So they continued to make the long drive to work and to complain about it. They also continued to let Sara take care of them.

One morning Sara saw Cousin Vera and Leon off to work and Uncle Ted off to his draughts game. With a sigh of relief, she sat down to drink her tea and eat a thick slice of spinach bread with a perfectly poached egg on top.

Having breakfast all by herself was one pleasure she still enjoyed. She was just stirring sugar into her tea when the door opened and Vera came in. Scotty, a dog who knew which people he wanted in his house and which ones he didn't, rushed forward yapping and snapping at Vera's feet.

"We've had a flat tyre. The car is still sitting right outside. You'd think you would have noticed."

Now Sara was much too glad to see them leave to stand by the window gazing after them, so she said nothing.

"Leon's changing the tyre and he's going to be late, so

I'm calling a cab for myself. Drat that dog!" Vera exclaimed, tripping over Scotty. "Really, Sara, that nasty mutt has to go!"

Sara felt sick. She had known Vera since they were children. She knew that once Vera got an idea she never gave it up. By the time Vera's cab had arrived and she had left for the day, the blackest mood of her life had settled on Sara Fisher.

By midmorning, the children next door saw her wrestling with clothes as she hung them on the line.

Karen and Edward came over and sat on the picnic table beside the clothes-line to talk to her.

As Sara fought her way out of a large shirt belonging to Leon, she found herself telling the children about the changes in her house and her life.

"And now Scotty! I know Uncle Ted dislikes him. He tries to kick him when he thinks I'm not looking, and Leon keeps saying he's a stupid dog. Of course, Scotty isn't the smartest dog in the world, but he's such good company."

Sara moved on to a nightgown of Vera's that seemed impossibly knotted.

"I wish we could help," Edward said.

"What she needs," said Karen, "is that, that – oh, you know, that word that starts with a 'd'."

"A dragon?" Edward asked.

"A bigger dog?" Sara Fisher suggested.

"A drama?"

"A drastic measure?"

Karen stomped her foot.

"I'm talking about Hector, Edward."

"Of course! I think you're right. Oh, Miss Fisher, Hector can take care of everything!"

"Yes," Karen continued. "I can't remember exactly what he is, but we can lend you Hector."

"Lend me Hector? What on earth are you two talking about?"

"You know how you lent us the sugar? And our dad always lets Mr Campbell use our hedge trimmers. Well, Mother says that's what good neighbours do," Karen explained.

"Hector is a –, a –. It'll come to us. But I'm sure Hector's the answer. We'll go and get him."

As the children climbed off the table and raced for home, Miss Fisher was untangling a pair of red longjohns belonging to Uncle Ted. With only three extra people in the house, there seemed to be ten times as much laundry.

Leon's shirts were the worst; they were about the size of tablecloths and he wanted them washed and ironed by hand.

By midafternoon, Sara Fisher had the laundry hung on the line, the house cleaned, a stew simmering on the stove, and a shopping list made out.

Below a neat list of groceries to be bought, she had written:

> *– pick up Uncle Ted's prescription*
> *– take Leon's brown shoes to be re-soled*
> *– collect Vera's special order from*
> *Dagstein's Department Store*
> *– buy stamps*

Two months ago I would only have had to buy stamps, she told herself.

Before she left, she put Scotty on his lead and fastened it to the metal ring in the garden. With so many things to do, she could easily be later than the others in getting home. She didn't want to leave Scotty where they were likely to be.

"Miss Fisher! Miss Fisher!"

She looked up to see Edward waving to her from next door.

"Oh, Edward, keep an eye on Scotty, will you?"

"Sure, I like to talk to him. And, Miss Fisher, it's all settled. Hector's coming over this afternoon!"

"That's good. Thank you," she called, thinking about whether to begin at the chemist or the shoe repair shop.

Those two were nice children. She and Scotty enjoyed their company, but sometimes their games were impossible to follow. Hector? She knew very well they didn't have a dog. Anyway, it would take a remarkable dog to move Uncle Ted and Vera and Leon.

By the time she reached the chemist to pick up Uncle Ted's prescriptions, she was reminding herself that she **did** have all that room. Of course, she also had time for things like washing and cooking and shopping, not that they were what she enjoyed most, but perhaps she was being selfish. She decided she might be willing to help her relatives, but she had to draw the line when they wanted to make Scotty's life miserable. On the other hand, what was she going to do to get rid of the three of them?

By the time Sara Fisher had checked off all the errands on her list, the afternoon was almost over. She speeded up her steps when she emerged from the grocery store to find dark clouds piling up in the western sky.

"Oh, dear, I hope it doesn't rain before I get home."

"You'll need to hurry," said a shopkeeper who was standing in his doorway looking at the changing sky.

Even though she was weighed down by her many packages, Sara reached home before the storm broke. She ran into the house to drop her bundles on the kitchen table, intending to go straight outside to get Scotty and the clothes. She had reckoned without Uncle Ted, however, who came storming into the kitchen.

"He put me out of my room! He put me out of my room! Did you ever hear the like? He just picked up all my things and put them out in the hall and moved himself in. Have you ever heard anything so outrageous?"

Well, yes, I have, thought Sara Fisher, remembering that Uncle Ted had moved her out not so long ago. But to her uncle she said, "Who? What has taken your room?"

"He say he's Hector. He says he's your guest, but there's no room for him. You'll just have to put him out."

"Hector? Oh!" Sara suddenly remembered the children, those nice, friendly children from next door. This morning she had been so caught up in her worries she had hardly paid attention to them. She seemed to remember they had wanted to help. She knew they had said something about Hector, but wasn't Hector some sort of dog?

"Whoever he is, he can't stay. The idea of moving a man's possessions out of his room, right out of his room!"

"I'm sure there's some mistake. I'll take care of it, Uncle Ted," Sara said. "But first, I must take the washing off the line. You didn't by any chance bring in the wash?"

"Wash? What? Oh, the washing. No, no, I haven't seen it."

"Well, **I** must see it. Just wait a moment, and then I'll try to sort out what's happening here."

In the garden, Miss Fisher was greeted by a joyously barking Scotty. She spoke to him, patted his head, and began a whirlwind progress down the clothes-line, transferring the dry clothes to a large wicker basket.

She hadn't emptied more than half the line before the back door slammed and Vera strode across the lawn, looking darker and more threatening than the cloud-filled sky.

"What do you mean by inviting a guest when we are here? You know we are doing our best to find an apartment in the city. This is a difficult time for us. No one wants to make that long trip to work each day. How can you show so little concern for us?"

Vera was almost foaming in anger.

"What's the matter?"

"'What's the matter?' she says. My father has been put out of his room and when Leon spoke to this Hector

person, the impudent intruder told him to pack and
get out!"

"Are you saying Hector told Leon to pack or that Leon
told Hector?" Sara asked, confused over the identity of
the impudent intruder.

"Honestly, Sara! This Hector person has ordered Leon
to leave!"

Sara pushed a stray curl back from her forehead and
looked around for some means of making sense of this
new nonsense in her life.

"I'm afraid I don't quite know who this Hector –"

"HA!"

Both women jumped as they turned to find Leon
behind them.

"And ha-ha," he added. "So you don't know this
Hector!" Turning to his wife he added, "After you left, he
told me to go away because he was busy watching Sara
from the window. 'Poetry' he called her. He says he's
staying forever." Turning back to Sara, Leon said, "You
might have told us you were getting married."

"You could have introduced us," Cousin Vera added.
"You could have warned us. You could have given us
time to find a place. You could –"

"We've found a place. I've decided we'll take the
apartment we looked at," Leon said. Turning on his heel,
he left.

"– have fallen in love with someone other than an
unmannerly boor!"

Vera wheeled round and followed her husband.

Sara had the impression that her back door had turned into the lid of a jack-in-the-box. She glanced over to see who or what would pop out next. When nothing more happened, she sank on to the bench of the picnic table, still holding a half-folded sheet in her arms.

"What is going on?" she asked Scotty.

He wagged his tail.

"Oh, I agree that it's good, but I don't understand it."

She finished filling the clothes basket, looped Scotty's lead over her arm, and started back to the house.

Uncle Ted, who had been watching for her, opened the door, not to let her in but to say, "They're leaving! Vera and Leon are leaving! Can't you do something about Hector Whoever?"

"That's just it, Uncle Ted," Sara said, managing to squeeze past him into the kitchen. "I don't know what's going on! But it doesn't sound like a tragedy. Weren't Vera and Leon going to take an apartment and leave anyway? Why don't I serve supper, and we'll all sit down and talk this over?"

"We are not staying for supper," Vera said, popping into the kitchen, carrying a small suitcase. "Leon is loading the car and we'll send for the rest of our things. Thank you for everything!" she concluded in a tone that clearly meant, "Thanks for nothing!"

"Wait, Vera. Maybe Leon and I can handle this Hector. I'm sure that together –"

"No, Father, Leon has been insulted enough. **You** handle Hector."

"By George, I will!"

Uncle Ted headed for the stairs.

"Good-bye, Sara," Vera said, collecting a sack of Sara's groceries under her free arm before she left, slamming the door behind her.

In the silence that followed, Sara Fisher untangled Scotty's lead from the table leg and unsnapped it from his harness. Immediately, Scotty headed for the stairs and began barking as he climbed.

Almost simultaneously, shouting and the sound of running feet were added to the noise of barking.

"Now what?" Sara asked of no one at all.

Uncle Ted raced downstairs panting. "I'm taking a room at the tavern for tonight. Tomorrow I'll move in with Vera and Leon."

"What happened?" Sara asked. She seemed to be the last person to know what was going on.

"A young ruffian throwing me out of my room is one thing, but when he starts breathing purple smoke and shoots up ten feet high to poke his head through the ceiling, then this is no longer the place for me. Sara Fisher, I don't think you have any respect for your elders, letting a monster like that push me around."

Now it was Uncle Ted's turn to slam the front door. Just about the time he should have reached the front gate, the doorbell rang.

"We've come to get Hector," Karen told Miss Fisher. "We just saw the last one leave."

"Come in," said their dazed but grateful neighbour.

"He isn't going to want to leave," said Edward, who was carrying a small brass and bronze vase, mostly black with a long neck. "Why don't you two wait down here? It will make it easier."

"We don't let Hector out very often," Karen was saying, as Sara led the way back to the kitchen. "He always falls in love with someone and never wants to come back, but he has to obey the laws of the spell."

"Who is Hector?" Sara asked. "Or, what is Hector? I thought he was a dog or some sort of game you two were playing."

"Hector is a djinni. It always takes me the longest time to remember that word. You know, you **say** gee-nee, but it's **spelt** with a 'd'."

"A djinni?"

"Sure," Edward said, coming back with the bottle and with Scotty trailing happily behind. "He lives in here. Dad picked him up on a buying trip in the Middle East when we were just babies."

"He's great," Karen added. "He can take on human shape or, when he really needs to, he can look like a monster or he can breathe red, green, orange, purple or blue smoke."

"Yeah, if you ever need him again, just ask," Edward told a bemused Sara Fisher. "Mom says that's what neighbours are for."

It

is

an

equal

failing

to

trust

everybody,

and

to

trust

nobody.

ANONYMOUS

Whenever we had to pass the house, I'd concentrate on the low stone wall, a thick, solid wall, covered with a layer of rough concrete. On either side of the front path, the wall ended in a square column topped by concrete icing and a concrete ball as big as the globe in the school library. I looked at the wall because I wasn't afraid of it. I was terrified of the house.

Maybe most abandoned houses are like magnets to boys, but Credlow House was different. Even the oldest boys were scared, too scared to explore it in broad daylight.

"It's bad," Doug Grumber said. "My uncle was in it – to fix the electricity – a long time ago, before it got all overgrown like this. It gave him the creeps."

"My dad says there's a lift in there, something like a big wire cage. He says you can just about stand the house, but that lift'll kill you," Bill McIntosh added.

Driving past in the car, I had sometimes looked at the house quickly through the window. Credlow wasn't a mansion, just a big, two-storey house with a porch across the front. What made it worse than other empty houses? I didn't know, but it **was** worse. Long, trailing, thorny-looking weeds grew in front of it. Its blank windows stared blindly at the world, and its wall, still a greyish white, seemed to be hugging an evil secret.

"Are you afraid?" I asked my brother Dave.

"Nah!" he shook his head, then quickly added, "I'm not saying I'd go in there. It's not safe. You'd probably fall through the rotting boards and get crushed on the basement floor."

From the time I was four or five until I was eight, I guess all of us, the boys in the neighbourhood, were pretty equally scared of Credlow. The change came during the year I turned eight.

That summer Don Morris and Bill McIntosh, who were eleven and twelve, decided to go rafting down Big Stony Creek. My brother Dave wanted to go. I don't know anything else he ever wanted so badly. Five of them, the older boys, talked about nothing else for weeks. They went on and on making plans. I wasn't in on it. I mean, I knew from the start I couldn't go, but my mother let Dave go on talking just like he was going to get to go.

Then one day right out of nowhere, she said, "Dave, you can't go rafting. Big Stony Creek's not safe, and you know Mickey's too young to go."

"What's Mickey got to do with it?" Dave asked, staring

at me in disbelief.

"He's too young, and I'm keeping him here. You'll have to stay out of it too."

Dave argued. He told her that I didn't care about missing the trip, that I'd never been part of the plans, that it wasn't fair. I tried telling her too. I said I didn't want to go, didn't mind staying home. But her mind was made up.

I could see what was going on. When you're the younger kid, you always **see**, but there's nothing you can do anyway. Mom had just plain changed her mind, but she was making it sound like it was because of me.

In the end only three of the boys went rafting, and Dave wasn't one of the three. Nothing happened to them. They were fine.

I was the one who wasn't fine. Dave hated me. It wasn't sudden, but it wasn't all that slow either. I had always been a part of his crowd even though we were three years apart, but now I began to see I wasn't wanted.

"Uck! This kid stinks. Don't you ever give him a bath?" Doug asked Dave one day.

Before the trip to Stony Creek, Dave would have stood up for me. Now he just laughed. And it got worse. He didn't merely let the others take jabs at me, he did it too. He led the whole crowd in poking fun at me.

I guess I was pretty stupid. I kept trying to laugh it off. I **liked** these guys. They'd been my friends all my life. I guess I thought Dave didn't really mean it. I was waiting for them to get over it.

Then Dave thought about Credlow. He started to tease me about being scared of an old, ramshackle house.

Doug and Bill found more stories to tell about people whose hair had turned white just from going through the door, about horrible sounds that came from the basement, about big dogs whose hair would stand on end when they passed Credlow.

"Look how scared he gets just listening to us talk," they'd say, pointing at me.

"Place must be overrun with rats," Bill said. "So, Mickey, how come all the cats stay away? Because even they know it's haunted."

"Just walk in the house," they'd taunt me, after they had made it sound as awful as they could. "Prove you're not a scaredy-cat. Go inside."

Of course I didn't, and they made that an excuse for keeping me out of whatever they did for the rest of the summer. I played with Joey Welch and Tim Harrow, but I had a pain in my chest that wouldn't go away.

If, by chance, I ran into Dave with his friends, they would start talking about haunted houses, chicken kids, and what was going to happen to me when I went into Credlow.

"That house is waiting for you, Mickey. It's going to swallow you up," Doug told me.

"Look at him. He's scared stiff."

"Yeah, he's as white as that wall."

I saw the look on Dave's face, and the hurt in my

chest got worse.

Somehow that summer ended. I was in primary school while Dave and his friends were in secondary school. Although we went on different buses, they would get to the bus stop just before our bus came. Every day they'd do something to me, like make me trip, or take a paper I was supposed to turn in for maths class, or get ink on my shirt. If I had been dumb before, I guess I was just plain stupid now. I still couldn't hate my brother. I thought he was great, and I felt really bad that he didn't like me anymore.

One day on my bus, Kirk Nelson said, "What a bunch of jerks! Who's that big creep who shoved you into the side of the bus?"

I got up and moved without speaking to Kirk. That "big creep" had been Dave.

I kept thinking things would change, and about the middle of October, they did. We got our pumpkin to make a jack-o'-lantern and started planning our Hallowe'en costumes. Mom said something about our going trick or treating, and Dave made a face at me. I understood him to mean he wasn't taking me along with his crowd.

Fine, I thought. *I'll go with the younger kids.*

But a couple of days later he asked me about my costume, offered to lend me his blue and white bandanna, and told me he and the others wanted me to go trick-or-treating with them.

Nobody heckled me at the bus stop, or at least not

much. Dave and his friends occasionally spoke to me.
And I was going out with them on Hallowe'en. Sure,
things weren't like they used to be, but they were better
than they'd been recently. Dave was getting over being
mad at me. Someday everything would be just like
before. My chest didn't feel so tight, and I was pretty
happy with the world.

I overheard Dave's friends talking about a party after
trick-or-treating, but they didn't seem to be including me.
That was okay. They could have their party. I was glad
to be going out with them.

The younger kids went out right after supper. Dave
and his friends met at our house and hung around until
it was completely dark. Maybe their behaviour was
suspicious. Maybe I should have guessed something was
up. But if they were acting funny, I didn't notice.

Some of the group had torches. I started out with one,
but when Dave asked for it, I was pleased to be able to
give him something. We walked from one house to the
next, from one block to the next, farther and farther,
until I no longer knew where we were. Two or three
times I found myself pushed aside, missing out on treats
at a door. It didn't matter; I had plenty.

Then we came to a house with a low wall.

"Hey! This looks like –" I began.

"There's a jack-o'-lantern on the porch," someone
cried. "They're expecting us!"

"Where are we?" I asked.

"It's okay. I know these people," Don told me.

"Let Mickey through, you guys. You keep pushing my brother aside," Dave said.

In the middle of the pack, I approached the front door. I tried to see the house, but there were boys on all sides of me.

I couldn't see the front door, but someone in front of me was knocking.

"Open your bag," the guys told me. "We'll let you go first."

As I looked down and opened my sack for treats, I heard the door open and felt the two people in front of me move aside. I was grabbed on both sides, pushed hard from behind, and propelled through the open door where I fell on to a bare floor. Behind me the door slammed shut. I scrambled up, spilling the candy I had collected, and looked through a chink in the boarded-up window in time to see bobbing torch lights pass between stone columns topped by big concrete globes.

I knew where I was.

Confusion gave way to terror. I tried the door, but it was securely locked. I didn't yell, I think I was too scared to scream. I pounded on the door with the energy of panic, but it didn't budge.

They'll come back, I thought. *They can't leave me. Dave can't go home without me.* I stopped hitting the door and sobbed.

In the silence that followed, I heard a chuckle, just a soft, friendly laugh behind me.

My first thought was that they hadn't left me entirely

alone. At least one of the boys must have come in
with me.

"Wha –? Who's there?" I must have sounded like an
idiot. I spun round with my back to the door, wondering
what joke to expect now.

"I'm over here," someone said.

"Who are you?"

"I'm Johnny Reed. Who are you?"

"Mickey. My n-n-name's Mickey. If you're stuck in
here too, why'd you laugh at me?"

"'Cause I acted just like you when I saw I couldn't get
back out."

"Am I going to die in here?"

"I can get you out. But don't you want to look
around first?"

"It's pitch black in here. I can't even see you."

"Here," he said. His hand grasped mine. It was bigger,
so I guessed he was older. "Just stay beside me."

I sort of slid my feet along as I went because I was
sure I would trip over something or go falling through
a hole.

"Put your hand straight out in front of you," Johnny
told me. "That's the lift."

I reached out and touched metal bars. "I heard it's like
a cage, and that's what it feels like."

"There's nothing in there now. So you don't have to
be afraid."

"What used to be in it?" I asked.

(I told you I was stupid! I didn't really want to know,

not standing there in total darkness right in front of it.)

Johnny laughed again, kind of soft and still friendly.

"A long time ago a man locked someone inside the lift cage and then sealed up the house and went away for an ocean voyage. Maybe he was going to come back and get rid of the bones and no one would ever have known. But someone else came and found the skeleton. No one's been able to live in the house since. They tried painting and fixing and cleaning but nothing ever took away what happened. You're shaking a little. Are you scared?"

"A little. But not like when I thought I was alone here. Do you think there's a ghost? Is that what scares people off?"

"Oh, there's a ghost. That man who sealed up the house and went off to sea sank with his ship. The murderer's body was lost at sea, but he was so determined to come back here that his spirit returned. He has been trying to get into the house ever since."

"I wish you hadn't told me that."

Johnny chuckled again.

"Don't worry. Stick with me, Mickey, and that ghost won't come close."

"Can you get us out?"

"I'm pretty sure I know a way out."

"How did you get in?"

"Oh, just like you, I guess I trusted someone I shouldn't have."

We were still moving through the house, edging our

way along. Johnny seemed content to let me slide my feet along, although he appeared to be able to see better in the dark than I could.

"There's a window above the sink that isn't boarded up. It's too high to reach from outside. But you can crawl through, hold on to my hands, and drop to the ground."

Sure enough we found the kitchen window. Here there was even a little light from the moon which had now risen.

Johnny got the window open, held my hands after I'd crawled through, and lowered me as far as he could reach.

"What about you?" I called up to the window.

"I told you I'm not scared any more. Besides, I'm kinda waiting for somebody."

"The one you shouldn't have trusted?" He didn't answer. "I'm glad you were there," I said into the darkness.

"You're okay, kid. Here, take off that bandanna and hold it out. I want to toss you something for trick-or-treat. Here's a haunted house souvenir."

I did as I was told, called "Thanks", and stuffed the bandanna into my pocket.

Now all I wanted was to get home. Here at the back of the house the garden sloped away into an overgrown bramble, thick with stark, bare trees. At the foot of the slope I could see the street with streetlights and an occasional car. Heading for that distant street would be

the fastest way home. I didn't want to make my way
round the house anyway.

As I set off downhill, the brambles tore at my legs and
arms. The rough branch of a tree caught my shirt and
pulled it off. I didn't stop to get it. The faster I went the
more my fear came back to me. The more frightened I
became, the faster I went. I was racing down that hill,
not caring how badly scratched I was.

I was flying straight at the back wall when a man rose
up from the weeds, a dark, silhouetted figure.

I hadn't thought I could be more scared, but my heart
thudded so hard it seemed to be flip-flopping, like a fish
on land.

"No!" This time I did cry out.

"Take it easy there, boy. Johnny, is that you? You're
not afraid of your uncle, are you?"

"It's not … I mean, I'm not Johnny. He's up there.
He's in the house. Are you the one who locked him in?"

"In the house still, is he?" He stared towards the house
as though he had just thought of it. Turning back to me,
he seemed to see me clearly for the first time.

"You're only half dressed and it's chilly. Why are you
out at night like this?"

"I was trick-or-treating and … Look, I just want to get
home now."

"Here, I can help you over the wall."

He locked his hands and I stepped on them, grasped
the top of the wall and pulled myself up.

"If you're Johnny's uncle," I said, "you should get on

up to the house. I think he's waiting for you." The man gave a sort of groan. "He's got a right to be mad at you. He trusted you," I added, thinking more of Dave than of the man beside the fence. "But I don't think he's mad anymore."

The moonlight struck him full for a moment. He looked sick, a washed-out, old man in a damp brown coat. Then he turned away, and I jumped down to the other side of the fence.

Bareheaded and in my vest, I must have been cold, but I don't remember it. I'm not sure I even noticed.

Mostly what I felt was mad. *I'll never speak to Dave again,* I thought. *Who cares what his friends think of me? I've been in Credlow – and got out again, no thanks to them.*

If that place had really been abandoned, if Johnny hadn't been there, I'd still be there, crying and probably scared to death. I wouldn't have got out on my own.

By the time I reached home, Dave was back too. He looked pale, and my parents were tight-lipped and angry-looking.

"Did he leave you?" my dad asked.

I looked at Dave, and he looked away. This was my chance. He deserved everything that was coming to him.

I looked back at Mom and Dad and said, "I just got separated from the others."

Alone in our room, Dave said, "I didn't go to the party at Doug's house. I told Dad that I thought you were in Credlow. If you hadn't got here when you did, I'd have told him everything. Honest, Mickey, I'm –"

I didn't want him to say what he was about to say, so I said, "It's nothing, Dave." I wasn't mad anymore, but I wasn't sure what I did feel. I thought that if Johnny Reed could forgive an adult who had left him in that scary house, I could forgive my dumb brother.

Getting ready for bed, I found the bandanna in my pocket, handed it back, and turned away. I didn't bother to say thanks. I knew that I didn't owe Dave any thanks for his help with my Hallowe'en costume.

"What's this?" he cried out.

"What?" I asked, turning round. And then I remembered. "Oh, a boy named Johnny gave me a treat, a souvenir from Credlow House. You can have it."

"Johnny! Do you mean Johnny Reed?" Dave shrieked.

"Yeah, that was his name. Do you know him?"

"Mickey, don't you know that it was Johnny Reed who was locked in the lift cage? His uncle shut him up in the house forty years ago!"

I guess the one thing Dave and his friends had failed to tell me about Credlow was how it had come to be haunted.

I was facing him now, and I could see the finger bone lying on the bandanna; above it, Dave's white, staring face; and, in the mirror behind, my own round eyes.

Whatever Dave told his friends about me must have been pretty impressive because they all began to treat me like someone special. But no one ever asked me about that night in Credlow. Sometimes I could see they were curious, but I guess they were embarrassed too. That's okay; I'd just as soon not talk about it. Sometimes, though, I wonder if the ghost of Johnny's uncle will ever make its way back to the house. Even dead and drowned, the old man's scared. I guess he thinks he'll get back from Johnny what he gave.

By spring, Dave was asking my advice about a climbing expedition he was going on with a club he belonged to. I was getting used to having him and his friends treat me like I was not just different but also a little better than they were.

Those guys thought I'd faced the scariest thing on earth and walked away. They were right about that; they were just wrong about what it was. They couldn't imagine anything colder or weirder than a ghost, but I hadn't known Johnny Reed was a ghost, or his uncle either. Just the same I **was** scared that night at Credlow.

Haunted houses can send chills down your spine, but there's nothing – in life or after – half as cold as hate.

We

require

to

extend

our

ideas

of

the

space-time

continuum

still

farther.

ALBERT EINSTEIN

One of the earliest pictures of Jared, after his baby pictures of course, showed him with his arm around the neck of a sturdy brown dog who looked, with dignity, right into the camera. Around the two of them, the toddler and the dog, were several roly-poly puppies. Both Jared and the puppies were covered with dust from the dry, grassless area around the dog kennel.

Nick, who was Jared's companion in the picture and also the dark, handsome father of the litter of puppies, was a part of Jared's childhood, always there and always the standard against which Grandpa compared the new puppies.

"That puppy'll never be a patch on Nick," Grandpa used to say.

None of them ever measured up, even the occasional fine pup that Grandpa chose to keep. At some point in between Jared's visits to his grandparents' farm, Nick came to the end of a long, splendid life. Eventually, there was only one dog left, a son of Nick.

"No, he's not much like Nick," Grandpa would say.

He must have said it many times over the years because Jared always thought of it when he looked at Monty, a dog who was named after a general but who had no fighting spirit, according to Grandpa. Jared couldn't help wondering what had made Nick so special.

Just the same, seeing Monty was one of the things Jared looked forward to when visiting his grandparents. "Treasure hunting" was another. Like most children, Jared dreamed of digging for buried treasure, but at his grandparents' house the dream could become a reality. Grandpa's farm sat on a piece of land that had been in active use since long before Columbus reached America. Indians had lived on this fertile stretch of the stream still known by its tribal name. Jared knew all about the Indians; Grandpa had explained about them the first time he showed Jared the coffee tin filled with arrowheads found on the farm. Together with stone hammerheads, these were the most common finds. Jared had even found a few himself. These were one kind of treasure, but there were others.

Buttons and coins could be turned up too, and these certainly hadn't belonged to Indians. Some were German.

"Hessian," Grandpa explained. "People who were paid to fight for the British in the Revolutionary War."

Other items came from the Civil War.

"There's a cemetery over that hill that's filled with the graves of Union soldiers from a battle fought nearby, nothing big enough to get into the history books, just a skirmish. Maybe it was fought right here."

Sometimes when Jared was helping with the ploughing, he and Grandpa found bullets, which made it clear that some shooting had taken place on that land. Digging up the past was one of the best things about being with his grandparents.

The year he was ten, Jared was walking with Grandpa and Monty, who was grown but not really old, along the Socodoquinet Creek, which ran through the farm.

"The Indians believed the water could cure you, speed up the healing of wounds. See that?" Grandpa stopped and knelt on the bank to point to a muddy swirl in a shallow section of the creek.

Jared knelt beside Grandpa while Monty splashed out into the water stirring up reddish-brown mud.

"First the Indians used that mud from the creek's bed to plaster over wounds, then soldiers from the Revolution, and then men wounded in the Civil War. I guess my old Nick was the last one to find out its secret."

Jared had thought he knew all about Nick. Nick had been the bravest, handsomest, finest dog ever. Despite all he remembered and all he'd heard over the years, Jared knew nothing about Nick and the mud.

"How did Nick find the secret?" he asked.

"Nick used to roam into those woods over there, and once in a while he'd run foul of a pack of wild dogs.

He'd fight like a real demon, that Nick, but what could he do against a dozen or so wild animals?

"More than once he got so chewed up that I thought there was no hope for him. But you know what he'd do? He'd roll in this mud, get coated with it, and the darned stuff would heal him. Not right away, but over time. Over time, it would," Grandpa repeated.

Jared leaned over and ran his fingers through the mud. It felt just like ordinary mud.

"What happened to Nick?" Jared asked, realizing that there must be one more story he hadn't heard.

"The dogs finally got him," Grandpa said. He sat staring into the water, and for a minute Jared thought he wasn't going to say any more.

Then with a sigh he went on. "One evening he didn't come home and I went out looking for him. He was right over there. See, just under that big maple. I almost didn't recognize him. One ear was torn. An eye was slashed. He was cut right through to the bone on a front leg. I thought he was dead then, but after a bit I could see he was still breathing.

"Well, I didn't think he had a chance. But I carried him as far as this mud; and, by golly, he managed to roll himself in it. With some help from me he got covered with it.

"For two days he lay there, and I'd check on him each day. He was getting well – even after the wounds he had suffered."

"But what happened to him? Didn't he get well after

all?" Jared couldn't help asking.

"The wild dogs came back to the creek. Oh, they were bold in those days. I heard them, and I got my rifle. When I reached the creek, I couldn't believe my eyes. Five or six wild dogs with muzzles covered with blood and foam were fighting what looked like a mud creature. Nick had somehow got on to his feet – and he was fighting. That dog didn't know how to quit. I fired right into the pack, and they cleared out. But it was too late for Nick. A second battle was too much; he was dying when I reached him."

Monty came up shaking off water, and Jared stretched his hand out and rubbed the dog's head, his thoughts on the dog he still remembered, a lost part of his own past.

In the early spring of the following year Jared made the biggest find of his life. Even Grandpa said it was the best ever. On a Saturday afternoon, with some help from Monty, he was digging a circular flower bed for his grandmother. A lifetime of experience had taught Jared to look at each spadeful of dirt.

He was letting the soil slide off when he saw the glint of something metallic. Quickly he picked it up and rubbed it on his jeans. It wasn't exactly round, and it was larger and heavier than any coin he had ever seen.

Calling as he ran, Jared took the find to his grandparents.

"There's writing on it," he said when his grandfather met him.

"I have to get the magnifying glass."

Examining it under the glass, all three could see that the writing was not English.

"It's German," Grandma said. "I can tell that much, but I don't know what it means."

"What's this for?" Jared asked, pointing to a sort of slit in the object.

"That's for a ribbon because this is a medal. That's what it is!" Grandpa exclaimed.

After supper Jared sat on the porch with his grand-parents talking about the find and drinking lemonade as the day ended.

"What's that noise?" Jared asked, as a sound from the distance reached them.

"The dogs," Grandpa said shortly.

"The **wild** dogs?" Jared asked, instantly remembering the story of how Nick died. "I thought they were gone a long time ago."

"Sometimes all of us around here try to get rid of them, but after a time there are more of them. In a pack like that they're as dangerous as anything you could meet in the woods."

"And this latest bunch is getting bolder," Grandma added.

Instead of being satisfied with the medal he had found, Jared wanted more than ever to hunt for the farm's buried treasure. Wherever he sank a shovel he seemed to be digging into history. Before his parents picked him up the next afternoon, Jared had doubled the size of the flower bed but without finding anything else of interest.

More than two months passed and school had ended before Jared came back to stay with his grandparents. This time he brought a suitcase for his annual two-week visit.

Little green plants were coming up in the flower bed he'd dug. Grandma was pointing to them before the car even stopped.

"My new flower bed is going to be beautiful," she told Jared and his parents.

Grandpa joined them and invited everyone to come round the back of the house to see what he'd just dug up. They found it on the back steps: a large curved bone with teeth, big teeth, in it.

Jared tentatively touched the curve of the bone and, just for a second, he thought of dinosaurs.

"What is it?" he asked.

"Jawbone of a mule. A big, fine animal. Who knows how long it has been in the ground."

"Maybe it came from the Civil War," Jared's father suggested.

"Or it may have belonged to the mill owner who built this house around the time of the Revolution."

After lunch when his parents had left, Jared went back outside to get reacquainted with the land. Monty joined him in a circuit of the big field beyond the creek.

The two of them had reached the far edge of the

newly planted acreage when they heard the dogs. The baying sounded far away and not much different from the last time Jared had heard it – the day he had found the medal.

The fur on Monty's back bristled, and Jared stepped up the pace, not out of fear but as a precaution. He and his parents had also talked about the dogs after his last trip to the farm. "Nothing's more dangerous," his dad had said, echoing Grandpa's judgment.

Something changed in the barking of the dogs. They picked up a new, more urgent sound. In response, Monty growled and broke into a run, and Jared joined him. With relief he spotted the corner of the field and kept moving steadily along, knowing that each row he passed brought him that much nearer home.

As his feet pounded the soil, his heart pounded in his ears. He had already walked a long way before he heard the dogs, so he wasn't running at his peak speed. Ahead of him he could see Monty's hind legs and tail sailing over the ground.

We're both going to look pretty cowardly, he thought, *if we come flying into the house scared and breathless.*

He made up his mind to stop at the creek, catch his breath, and walk calmly back to the house. As the creek came into sight, waves of relief swept over him. Moments later the relief was succeeded by shame. The main danger, Jared told himself, had been to Monty. The wild dogs frequently killed small animals, including farm animals and pets. Several people, Grandpa had said, had been trapped by the animals but had got away. Still, Jared knew his fear had been for himself. The dogs could kill. If no one came in time, if nothing frightened them away, a pack of wild dogs would kill.

Monty waded into the water and drank deeply. The run had been hard on him.

"He only ran because I panicked," Jared told himself and decided to say nothing of his fears to his grandparents.

The next morning Jared was up early enough to help his grandmother fry sausages and make buttermilk blueberry pancakes for breakfast.

"Do you think it would be all right for me to dig on the other side of the creek? I want to find some more arrowheads while I'm here."

"Why don't you try around the maple? That land's never been cultivated, so there are likely to be some left there," Grandpa suggested.

After they had eaten, Jared collected a pick and a shovel and headed across the creek. At the edge of the lawn he whistled for Monty, but the dog didn't come and Jared didn't want to go looking for him.

Taking his grandfather's advice, Jared chose the area around the maple for digging and started by loosening the ground with the pick. Before long he had set a steady rhythm of plunging in the shovel, lifting it up, and tapping the dirt off gently so that he could look it over carefully.

In less than an hour he had found a broken piece of chipped stone that must certainly have been an

arrowhead. The discovery gave him new energy.
Watching each shovelful intently, he picked up the pace:
dig, lift, spill; dig, lift, spill.

Before long he glimpsed a flash of something white,
possibly a quartz arrowhead. He was bending over to
examine it when a sound caught his attention, and he
looked up. Pale brown eyes that were almost yellow
looked into his own.

In that instant he knew he was looking into the eyes
of a wild dog, and his heart gave a leap of fear. Carefully
he turned his head and looked to each side of him,
searching for the best way to run. Instead, he found
himself surrounded. He and the maple tree were at the
centre of a circle of silent, watching creatures, as
frightening as snakes and even more dangerous. These
ill-matched curs were the wild dogs. And for the
moment, it was a standoff.

Jared gulped air and only then realized he hadn't been
breathing. The word "help!" screamed through his mind,
but his voice wouldn't work.

He had never in his life imagined that dogs could be
so terrifying.

He realized he was still holding the shovel, gripped it
tighter, and raised it over his head. If he had to fight, he
would fight. He began swinging it in a circle, trying to
keep them off from all sides.

From a great distance, he heard a canine howl of rage.
Across the creek, at the top of the slope to the house,
Monty was in the garden by the fence. He was doing

more than complaining; he was also running. Jared felt a surge of gratitude for the dog's loyalty even as he saw that Monty could never reach him in time.

Waving the shovel in the air, he kept turning, trying to keep all the wild dogs in sight. Eyeing him warily but relentlessly, the dogs began to move in, slowly at first. Jared had time to wonder if Grandpa might be coming to call him to lunch. Then with a burst of speed so quick Jared didn't even see him, the first dog struck. His teeth cut right through the denim of Jared's jeans. In the shock and pain of the attack Jared almost dropped the shovel. Knowing it would be a disaster to lose his only weapon, he held on and swung at the head of the attacking dog. Shovel and head met with a crack, but the dog didn't let go of the leg he was fastened on. As though on signal, the rest of the pack rushed Jared at once. Pain made his sight blur.

This is it, Jared thought. *I can't fight them off.*

Even if someone heard the attacking dogs or if Monty's alarm could bring help, help would come too late. No one could reach him in time. Grandpa had been too late to save Nick. No one was coming to save Jared.

Beyond the heaving mass of savage beasts rushing at him, he caught sight of one more dog. Although it had arrived late, this one, battle-scarred and filthy, looked fiercer than all the rest of the pack. Maybe this was the leader. Jared was taking wilder and wilder swings, rapidly losing out to the dogs, when he saw that this last animal did not belong to the group. As he swung at the inner circle, the new dog attacked from the outside, ripping flesh from bone and sending yelping dogs flying to the underbrush from which they'd emerged.

In the agony of the mass attack on his legs, Jared began to fall to his knees and one of the wild dogs launched himself and bit right at the bone of Jared's forearm. No longer able even to swing at the dogs, Jared knew his fate was up to the strange, fierce creature that had come to fight for him.

Quickly reducing the pack to two die-hard attackers, the new dog went for the throat of the animal whose teeth held Jared's arm, and the last two wild dogs turned on the scarred, dirty intruder.

An outburst of raucous barking drew Jared's eyes towards the creek. Late, but there at last, was Monty, making enough noise for the whole U.S. Cavalry.

Just before he passed out, Jared thought he heard Grandpa calling his name.

By midafternoon Jared lay quietly in bed, pale but still conscious. Both his arm and leg had required stitches. He had been bandaged, given injections, and sent to bed to sleep as much as possible. Now Grandpa sat beside him talking, talking about his fear, about Jared's courage in driving away all the dogs, about the unexpected bravery of Monty who had charged into the fight like a mad bull.

"I guess he does have a bit of Nick's spirit after all," Grandpa was saying.

Jared was glad Grandpa had found something to

praise in his old friend Monty, but his own curiosity was too great to ignore.

"Who was the other dog, the first one that helped me?"

"Other dog? There was just Monty and then me. You drove the rest of the pack away yourself."

"No, I didn't. I tried with the shovel, but once I was bitten I couldn't really swing at them. It was the black dog that drove them away. He was still there when Monty came. You must have seen him."

"I saw Monty reach you and the last of those miserable scroungers slink away. There was only you and Monty and those two curs. I could see you clearly, and I was running as fast as I could but you fell before I reached you."

Grandpa kept talking and Jared felt himself beginning to drift off. His last conscious thoughts were of his rescuer. He saw the dog, like Monty, only black. Or no, maybe not black, maybe mud-covered. Dripping mud and a little stiff-legged, the avenging dog had hurled himself into that circle of death.

Consciousness slipped into dream as Jared saw first the menace of a face with yellow-brown eyes that – in the way of dreams – was supplanted by another face, this one with a single eye glowing with courage. The other eye in the dark face was closed by a long, ragged gash.

Jared smiled at the battered face and slept deeply.

The

only

gift

is

a

portion

of

thyself.

Ralph Waldo Emerson

THE GHOST OF FIDDLER'S ELBOW

"See, it doubles back on itself," Uncle Fred explained. "It's just the lie of the land here. The stream bends the way a fiddler bends his arm to hold his bow."

Marcy and Colin stood looking down on the rushing waters below them. Sutkins Creek, it was called. But this point where the stream passed then bent double and came back again, was known as Fiddler's Elbow.

They had come out to answer a question, walked through the light rain – several degrees above freezing. Now that they'd heard the answer to their question, the explanation didn't seem to be enough. They stood staring at the water, waiting for more. At last Colin said, "What about the ghost?"

Uncle Fred shook his head and flopped one hand at them. "No such thing as ghosts," he said dismissively. "Now I'm going straight on across there to the barn. Do you want to come with me or do you want to go on back to the house?"

Marcy would have liked to go on to the barn, but Colin wanted to go back to the house. Because he had a cold, she gave in.

Feeling a little let down, they watched their uncle follow the crest of the hill back towards the barn. They had come out to hear the story of Fiddler's Elbow, and all they had done was to look again at the funny loop of the stream.

Instead of snow, they had a misting rain for Christmas. Instead of the ghost story they had been promised, they had heard how the area got its name.

"I bet there isn't any ghost of Fiddler's Elbow," Colin said disgustedly.

Older by eleven months, Marcy spoke from her superior experience, "I didn't expect a ghost; I just wanted a ghost story."

She was especially fond of ghost stories, and the ones she liked best were the ones about ghosts who haunted the same house, or place, or family, for generation after generation.

She had thought it would be great to meet a ghost who had also met her grandmother. But, of course, it wasn't going to happen. It was like all the promises that don't come true. Well, the ghost hadn't been a promise exactly. The ghost was just one of those things that sound better than they turn out to be.

"I don't want to go back along the path," Colin said.

"We could still catch up with Uncle Fred," Marcy suggested hopefully.

"Let's walk around the 'elbow' and follow the road back to Grandma's house."

Marcy agreed even though the hillside looked wet and slippery. In fact, it turned out to be a great deal worse than it looked. About halfway down she slipped, lost her footing, and slid to the bottom on the seat of her jeans. Scrambling up again, she could see that the road was much farther away than it had appeared from the top of the hill.

As Colin and Marcy reached the bend in the creek, they broke into as much of a run as the long grass and dead leaves would allow, but they were still about a hundred metres from the road when the light rain became a downpour.

We should have taken the path back, Marcy thought, but she didn't blame Colin. She had wanted more adventure. Getting caught in a rainstorm, however, wasn't what she had in mind.

Beside the creek was a bit of orchard that belonged to their grandmother. The two dodged between the trees to reach a fence beside the road that, like the creek, was known as Fiddler's Elbow.

"Get in!" someone called. "I saw you a-coming."

Marcy peered through the rain to see a horse-drawn buggy.

"Who is it?" Colin asked.

"He must be Amish," Marcy told him.

"Are you Amish?" Colin called out to the man in the wagon.

"Come on," he called back laughing. "I'll give you a ride up to the house."

Marcy and Colin knew all the rules about not going off with strangers but no rule had included horse-drawn wagons. Deciding it would be as easy to jump out again as it would be to climb in through the open sides, Marcy said, "Let's go."

Having come to the same decision on his own, Colin was in the wagon before she finished speaking.

"If you aren't Amish, why do you have a wagon?" Colin asked.

"Amish aren't the only ones to have wagons. This is a genuine U.S. mail wagon. Hadn't been a-raining so hard, you could have seen that for yourselves on the side. I'm not supposed to pick anyone up, but of course I always do in the rain."

"Doesn't the horse mind the rain?" Marcy asked, because she was always concerned about animals.

"Not the rain nor the snow nor the ice. Nothing I can think of is as dependable as Baskins and this wagon and me. Whoa! See here, we brought you safe home."

One more mad dash through the now-blinding rain took them to their grandmother's door.

"I was just telling Fred he should never have left you," Aunt Sylvia said, as she met them at the door with their baby cousin under her arm. "He and your dad are putting on waders to go and search for you. Run to the back porch and stop them."

By the time they'd reclaimed Dad and Uncle Fred and changed into dry clothes, Grandmother had gingerbread cookies ready to be decorated. In the rush of Christmas preparations, the wagon ride was forgotten. Twisting bags of icing, the children added eyes and noses and mouths to gingerbread men. Marcy gave one a red suit with white icing trimming and a white icing beard.

A wood fire burned in the kitchen stove where mulled cider simmered, adding its scent to the smell of the fir tree and the spices of the baking. Linda, Marcy's mom, sat by the stove, rocking Aunt Sylvia's baby.

"It's an old-fashioned Christmas house," Marcy said to her grandmother. "Can we sit round the fire and tell stories after supper?"

"Can we tell ghost stories?" Colin asked.

Grandmother looked thoughtfully from one to the other and said, "When I was a little girl, we always told ghost stories on Christmas Eve. I didn't think anyone did that any more."

"Well, we want to. We want a real, old-fashioned Christmas even if we don't have snow."

Grandmother turned over the bowl she'd been stirring, tumbling a large ball of golden dough on to a floured board, and began to flatten the dough. She handed Marcy a rolling pin and showed her how to press the dough out as flat as possible. Colin was allowed to climb on to a counter to get a big cookie jar off the top shelf. In Grandmother's kitchen, the top shelf was right up at the ceiling. When he emptied out the jar, cookie cutters of all descriptions spilled over the table.

Marcy chose a star shape and Colin took a Christmas tree.

"I think I'll start us off with a Christmas story while we finish up the cookies," Grandmother suggested. "When I was just a girl, we used to sell apples every autumn right out there on Fiddler's Elbow. My sister, brother, and I would sit out there with the baskets and collect the money. Every year my father – that's your great-grandfather – would store bushels of apples in the cellar so we'd have them all winter."

Colin was using a wreath-shaped cutter and Marcy switched to an angel cookie cutter as Grandmother slid the first tray of cookies into the oven.

"So what happened with the apples?" Colin asked.

"Just before Christmas, we three children would take another dozen or so baskets of apples up to the roadside and sell them. Well, one Christmas, Mr Kohler stopped and asked for some apples. My brother Davy told him the apples were fifty cents a basket, but Mr Kohler laughed and said he didn't have any money, but he had a strong hankering for some apples.

"My sister Jenny May said, 'You can have an apple.' But that wouldn't do; he wanted a whole basket.

"'I tell you what,' he said. 'You give me a basket of those apples and I'll give you a ride to school any time the weather's bad.'

"I had already made up my mind he was to have the

apples anyway, so I said yes."

"That's not much of a Christmas story," Colin said, "except for the fact that it happened at Christmas."

"That's because you haven't heard the end yet," Grandmother said.

Marcy looked the cutters over to make another selection. She liked sticking with one shape for at least a dozen cut-outs, but Colin had already cut a pig, a chicken, an owl, a moon, a heart, and even a whale.

"How can you make those things look like Christmas cookies?" she asked him, taking an elf-shaped cutter.

"We didn't know it," Grandmother continued, "but Mr Kohler's wife was sick. It turned out she almost died that winter, but at the time we didn't know why he wanted the apples. It seems all their money was going for the doctor's bills and medicine.

"After Christmas, when we went back to school in the one room schoolhouse, we all had to tell something we had been given for Christmas. One by one each of the Kohler children said they had been given stockings filled with apples and nuts. About that time word got round about how sick Mrs Kohler was, and all the farm families around here started to help.

"When somebody smoked hams, they left a ham for Mr Kohler. On baking day, there'd be an extra loaf of bread, or sometimes it would be eggs or a cake."

"That's a nice story," Marcy said. "Did Mrs Kohler get well?" She picked up an apple-shaped cutter for her next row of cookies.

"Yes, she did, but Mr Kohler never forgot us or that basket of apples."

Somehow supper was ready by the time the cookies were decorated. As soon as the meal was over and the dishes were washed, Grandmother set Marcy and Colin to work stringing cranberries and popcorn beside the fire in the living room.

"Can we hear ghost stories now?" Colin asked.

Toby, Aunt Sylvia's baby, had fallen asleep, but the rest of them sat by the fire and listened to the stories.

Uncle Fred told about two brothers who had to sleep in a haunted room in an old farmhouse. In the middle of the night, the ghost came and stood at the foot of their bed, "giving off a strange glow and smelling of the grave".

"You're going to make Colin and Marcy afraid to go to bed," their mother protested.

"No, he won't. I love ghost stories," Colin said.

"I wish we could see a **real** ghost," Marcy said.

"Didn't you say that Fiddler's Elbow is haunted? What did you start to tell us in the car?"

"Oh, the story is," Mother began hurriedly, having thought better of telling them about the haunting of the place they had come to visit, "that here where the river doubles back, time doubles back also. What has happened before may happen again."

"I have a ghost story," Dad said before Marcy could ask the questions that her mother's remarks had raised. He told a long story about a castle – far away and nothing like Grandmother's house – where steps were heard on the stairs each night.

"So eventually," he concluded, "the family grew so accustomed to the ghost that they'd each smile and nod and sometimes say 'Good evening' as they passed him on the stairs."

Soon after that Marcy and Colin got ready for bed. Colin settled down on a mattress in their parents' bedroom and Marcy went to bed on the camp-bed in the kitchen.

"Are you sure you can sleep here?" her grandmother asked for the fourth time. "I wish you'd take my bed and let me sleep in the kitchen. I'm always the first one up anyway."

"I wake up early too. I can help you when you come in to start breakfast. Can I help with more baking in the morning?"

"Oh, yes! I still have to make the eggnog cake, and we have to make orange-nut stuffing for the turkey. There will be lots of things you can do."

"Then I'll want to get up early and not miss any of it. Besides, I want to be here," Marcy assured her. "It's nice to fall asleep with people nearby."

"As long as we don't keep you awake," Grandmother said.

"I'm almost asleep already."

But Marcy had spoken too soon. On crisp white sheets, with the warm glow still coming from the wood stove, she lay awake, happily smelling dried apples and a lingering scent of cinnamon. She found she could hear the voices of the adults clearly over the crackle of the fire in the next room.

"I hope we didn't give the children nightmares from the ghost stories," Aunt Sylvia was saying.

They're wrong to think we're scared, Marcy thought. *I still wish I could see a ghost just once.*

"I could tell you didn't want them to hear about our Fiddler's Elbow ghost," Grandmother said. "I had it all started for them while we were working on the cookies, but luckily I didn't say a word about the ghost."

"That was just too close to home!" Mother said.

"What's the story? I've never heard that one," Uncle Fred said.

Then, of course, nothing could have persuaded Marcy to stop listening.

"When I was young," Grandmother began, "my brother, sister, and I gave some apples to a man who couldn't pay us for them. In return, he told us that when it was raining or snowing, he'd stop and pick us up and give us a ride to save us the usual long walk to school. He was as good as his word. Whenever the weather was bad, he'd be there waiting for us. We knew we could depend on him, and in rain or snow we looked for him. Well, I grew up and had been away from home for a few years before we came back here to live and raise our family.

"I was out walking one day, when I was expecting Sylvia. Before long I knew I had made a mistake; the baby was coming sooner that we had thought. In fact, the baby was on the way. I was out there on the road just opposite the bend in the river, and I heard a wagon. I was surprised to find there were still wagons around, but then I saw it was Mr Kohler. He stopped for me and drove me up to the house. After that came the race to the hospital and the baby's birth. With all the excitement, I didn't think to mention Mr Kohler until much later. That's when I learned he had died several years before. Of course, no one believed my story about getting a ride with a ghost."

"But we believe you," Marcy heard her dad say. "Before we were married, Linda and I were visiting here and went walking down beyond where the apple orchards used to be."

The steady sound of the wind, the warmth of the bed by the kitchen stove, and the voices in the next room began to blend for Marcy. She closed her eyes and found herself right away in a dream of walking hand-in-hand with her mother and grandmother along the creek called Fiddler's Elbow. Behind them she heard the sound of a horse approaching at a steady trot.

"We knew snow was coming," continued the voice that Marcy could no longer hear. "But it hadn't started and the weather seemed mild enough. We were just turning back when the clouds opened. A whole blanket of snow seemed to fall at once. Huge, blinding flakes were coating us and everything around. I thought we'd be lost out there. That's when we reached the road and found the old buggy waiting for us."

As she slept under the covers by the black stove in the kitchen, Marcy smiled at her dream.

"We accepted the ride and thought nothing of it," Marcy's mother took up the story, "until we got safely back to the house and told Mother about the man who had picked us up."

Uncle Fred snorted. "I'd like to believe in ghosts as much as the next person, but here you are right in the middle of Amish country. Plenty of people have horse-drawn buggies. In both cases, you probably just ran into a good Samaritan, not a ghost at all."

"You're forgetting that I knew Mr Kohler. I recognized him," Grandmother said. "But there is something more. When we were kids and Mr Kohler gave us rides, he was breaking the rules. You see, he was the postman for this district. He wasn't supposed to let anyone ride in that buggy. He always said rules are rules, but people are people and sometimes you have to bend a rule to do the human thing. I recognized Mr Kohler, and I recognized that mail buggy too."

"It was also a mail buggy that we rode in," Marcy's dad said. "And how many of those do you think are still around? The man said that nothing was as dependable as he and his buggy and that horse."

"I even recognized his horse," Grandmother added. "If I hadn't been so preoccupied with bringing you into the world, Sylvia, I would have known there was something strange about that ride. I hadn't known Mr Kohler had died, but his wagon had long been replaced and his old horse Baskins had been dead for years even then. I do believe that, just as Linda said, the land and the water and time itself double back here at Fiddler's Elbow."

Deep in her own dream, Marcy shivered again, not from cold and not from fear but from pure delight at a wish come true.

A

man

had

rather

have a

hundred

lies told

of him

than one

truth

which he

does not

wish

should

be told.

SAMUEL JOHNSON

C A N
Y O U
T O P
T H A T ?

Mary Ann had never liked Martin. Years ago when he first moved in next door, he had only been four or five. The first time Mary Ann saw him he was standing in her back garden where he had just pulled up two of her mother's iris plants. He probably thought he was picking flowers, but he pulled up the whole plants, bulbs and all.

The roots hung down below the bulbs as he held them up to show Mary Ann, and he grinned. She didn't like his round face or his piggy eyes. He went home dragging the plants, and she could hear his mother laughing and telling him how "cute" he looked.

But **they** hadn't laughed. Mary Ann decided that she and Jane and Matilda would ignore him. The "pig boy" she called him.

For the first few years he was always coming into her garden and asking to play, but every time he asked,

Mary Ann would say, "I don't want to play with you. I have Jane and Matilda."

He could never understand, but eventually he would go away, and then Mary Ann would play happily.

Once when Martin was six or seven, he knocked at her back door, hammering at it until Mary Ann opened it.

"My mother says we should play together."

That was a new way of asking his same old question.

"I don't want to play with you," she told him. "I like to play with Jane and Matilda."

"My mother says you should. She says it would be better."

Better for her, Mary Ann supposed she meant. Naturally she wanted to get the little beast out of the house for a while.

Mary Ann sent him back just the way she had all the other times. His mother was stuck with him as far as Mary Ann was concerned. She went back to playing Barbie dolls with Matilda and Jane.

When he was nine, Martin used to sit on her fence. It was his "horse", he said. By this time he wasn't so round or even piggy-eyed anymore, but Mary Ann still couldn't stand him. She said that Jane and Matilda agreed with her.

He would sit on the fence and call, "Mary Ann, Mary Ann, come and catch me if you can."

Sometimes she would say, "Of course I could catch you. You're sitting still." But most of the time she ignored him.

Once Mary Ann overheard Martin's mother talking to hers, apparently complaining because she wouldn't have anything to do with him. Her mother was saying, "No, I don't agree with you. We believe she'll grow out of it."

Did she mean grow out of hating Martin? *Not likely,* Mary Ann thought.

The summer they were about eleven, Martin went away to spend a month with his father. Mary Ann wished he would go away for the whole summer. It would have been better still if he'd gone to live with his father.

She had good times together with Matilda and Jane. They went swimming, rode bicycles, made up a code, and wrote letters in it. One afternoon they took an old tablecloth and a thermos of lemonade and some tarts made with cherries from a tree in Mary Ann's garden down to a far corner of the garden. They spread out the tablecloth under a tree beside the fence. A breeze was blowing and it was a good place to be.

Someone suggested telling stories. Maybe it was Jane, because she was the one who began. She said:

Once there was a princess who was imprisoned in a tower by an evil witch. At first the little princess cried and cried, and then stomped her feet and yelled, and finally she sulked and wouldn't say anything for one whole day.

One day the witch was visiting her and gloating over the great reward she expected to get as soon as the king could sell his castle to raise the ransom money. The princess looked into her evil eyes and said, "You are a heartless old witch to keep me trapped here."

Now the witch couldn't stand to hear that, even though it was true – or probably because it was true. Anyway, the witch flinched, which means she jumped a bit inside her green, wrinkly skin.

"Here, now, young princess, I'll make a deal with you. Make a friend before I return for my next visit, and I will set you free without any ransom."

Of course, it only sounded like a good offer; the princess was locked in a tower. Even the witch's servants who gave her food were not allowed to unlock the tower. The princess got her food by lowering and then raising a basket on a long rope. No one but the witch could get into the tower, which was so high no one could even see or talk to the princess.

But the princess didn't think of all these problems until the witch had left. She saw the difficulties afterwards, but she was so glad to have a chance to win her freedom she started looking for ways to get round the problems.

Finally, she thought of the cat she had seen at the base of the tower when the witch brought her there. Looking round her bare tower room, she saw the single woollen blanket the witch had provided to keep her warm. Quickly she set about unravelling it until the whole blanket was nothing but a pile of soft woollen yarn. The princess tossed the bundle of wool through the bars on the window, holding on to one end of the wool. Then she began to jiggle the wool. She did this for a long time before she felt a tug. The cat had come to play with the wool. When the cat no longer tugged the wool, the princess knew it had grown tired, so she pulled the wool back up again.

Several times a day she would toss it out and play with the cat.

Then on the third day, just before the witch was due to return, the princess lowered her basket for food, waited until the servant below gave a jerk on the rope to indicate that it was ready, then she pulled the basket way up high but didn't reach out to take the food. Instead, she lowered it again, food and all, and waited. She held the rope taut so she could feel vibrations from the basket and when she felt the basket rocking on the ground below, she began to raise it. This time when it was outside the bars of her window, she looked and saw that – as she had hoped – the cat was in the basket.

The princess reached out and pulled the cat into her room. The cat, who'd been frightened by the sudden ascent into the sky, began to purr and rub its head against the princess. At that moment, the old witch came into the room, took one look at the princess and the cat, went into a rage, and exploded in a puff of green smoke, leaving the door to the princess's tower room standing open.

The princess rushed out of the room and soon found her way to the castle, which her parents were just on the point of selling, having at last found a buyer who could pay enough to meet the ransom demanded by the witch.

The king and queen were so happy that they made the cat a knight of the kingdom, and he lived at court for the rest of his life.

"Now," the question began that was asked after any story was told, "can you top that?"

Mary Ann was still thinking when a voice from the tree above said, "I can."

It was Martin. He had got back from his father's and must have been hidden in the tree throughout the picnic.

"This party doesn't include you," Mary Ann said icily.

"Oh, yes, it has included me. I've been here all the time. And I can tell a better story than old Who's-it."

"Her name is Jane!" Mary Ann said angrily. "You could at least remember it."

Martin had been moving down through the branches of the tree until he was sitting on a limb just above her with his legs hanging down.

"I have a story, and I can top old Jane What's-it. Let me tell it."

Mary Ann sat still, looking round the tablecloth. "Okay, I guess it's all right. Matilda wants to hear it."

"Listen to this," he said, which Mary Ann thought was no way to begin a story. Martin said:

There was this girl and she looked okay on the outside, but she had no heart. In place of a heart she had a small lump of coal. To look at her you might not know it because she looked like a princess. She lived in a big house with her mother and father, and she had a garden full of fruit trees and flowers, and she owned one of every toy that was ever made. Also, she had this sort of soft, curly hair that lights up in the sunshine. She had long legs and could run like the wind. I guess you could say she was kind of skinny, but not in a bad way. I mean, to look at she was okay.

The only way you could know she had no heart was to look into her eyes. Oh, they looked good too – as long as they weren't looking at you. But when she looked right at you, you could see those eyes weren't all bright and full of laughter like you thought. They were cold and hard and looked just like the lump of coal she had for a heart.

In a cottage by this princess's house, there was another kid, somebody who was all alone like her, and he wanted to be friends. But this princess person whose name was Merrybelle always told him she already had friends.

The kid watched her every day and he saw she played all alone with these two made-up characters she called Janice and Melinda. You see, she'd do anything to keep from making a **real** friend.

She didn't need a witch in her life. She ran up the steps of the tower and locked herself in and threw away the key. And all she would ever say when someone came to let her out was, "Go away. I don't want you here."

"I knew you were horrible," Mary Ann interrupted, "and so is your story." He might have gone on, but she started to shout, "Stop it! Stop it! Go away!"

Finally, Martin slid out of the tree on his own side of the fence. Mary Ann kept shouting anyway, and someone was crying. *It must be Matilda,* she thought. *She always cries at sad stories.*

Mary Ann reached up to wipe the tears from her own cheeks.

. . .the

fatal

bellman

which

gives

stern'st

goodnight.

Macbeth

THE
BELL-RINGER

I can't say when I realized one of my twin cousins was a killer. The idea always seems to have been at the edge of my mind, just a little too fantastic to believe on those golden, once-a-year party days. Lloyd and Boyd had the good fortune to be born in the summer, which meant they could celebrate their birthday under the blue skies of the southwest with a fiesta.

When I was very young, those long tables covered in bright woven cloths and laden with strange foods seemed magical. Aunt Rosina was Mexican and she served foods that were exotic in my world of roast beef and fried chicken.

The year I was six and the twins were nine, I remember sitting under a tree with my plate of food long after everyone else had finished. One of the adults suddenly swooped down and took my plate, exclaiming over the amount of food I had left. I hadn't finished, but

I was too shy to tell her. I had thought those dishes had come out of a fairy tale, and I was trying to make them last as long as I could.

After a whole day of feasting and game-playing on the birthday shared by Boyd and Lloyd, we would be blindfolded with brightly patterned scarves to take turns attacking the piñata.

Before I was six, I never seemed to hit the piñata on my allotted turn. Then as I grew older, I began to hit it but never hard enough to break it. I was shy and gentle, happy on the fringes of my big cousins' parties. I was too timid to whack a piñata, too backwards to save a plate of food that was as good as a key to an enchanted land. I was also the only person in the world who suspected the deadly secret of my two bold, wonderful cousins. In short, I was the last person you'd ever expect to do anything about it. Maybe if I'd been bolder I would have acted sooner. But if I'd been bolder, I might have been in the thick of activities and probably wouldn't have seen what was happening.

My aunt and uncle lived in a large, sprawling, U-shaped adobe house, built around a courtyard. The end of the courtyard that wasn't enclosed by the house was surrounded by a high wall with big wooden gates. Beside the gateway was a tower with an old bell that my uncle claimed had come from the Alamo.

Just at dusk on their birthday each year, my cousins would start from opposite sides and scramble up the rough stone surface of the tower. The winner would

signal his victory by pulling the rope and ringing
the bell.

Though twins, my cousins were not identical. Lloyd
was taller, thinner, and darker, with black hair and shiny,
laughing black eyes. Boyd was thicker, fair-haired, and
often cruel to me. They both beat me in the games they
condescended to play with me, but Lloyd was always
nicer about winning. I didn't mind losing to him as
much. Boyd was a poor loser. I remember wondering
one year if Lloyd was letting Boyd ring the Alamo bell.
Lloyd seemed faster, but Boyd was more frequently
the winner.

Aunt Rosina was related to me only by marriage, but I
liked her better than my Uncle Jordan. Like Boyd, Uncle
Jordan liked to gloat when his sons won at games.
Sometimes he called me "little stick" because I was
skinny with long, bony legs.

Once when we were young, he caught Boyd under
one of his arms and me under the other, exclaiming,
"What a frail little thing you are! You need muscles like
my boys. Look, Angela," he called to my mother. "Leave
Hope with us. We'll soon see her looking fit and strong."

Mother just laughed and said she couldn't spare me,
but after that, Boyd began calling me "Hopeless", a
nickname I hated. Lloyd never heard the nickname
without frowning at his brother. Once, when the three of
us were alone, he told Boyd, "You ought to call her
Hope. Can't you see how stars shine in her eyes?" I think
I worshipped him a little from then on.

On the twins' twelfth birthday, the year I was nine, I moved out of the shadows to watch the race to the bell tower, and Uncle Jordan noticed me, clapped me on the back, and urged me to cheer along with everyone else. I was already learning that loud people are under the impression that everyone wants to be like them.

"Shout for one of them," Uncle Jordan said. "Who do you want to win? You can do it. Call out. Come on now."

At that moment I thoroughly disliked my uncle, but I let myself be bullied into saying faintly, "Yeah, Lloyd."

Uncle Jordan roared with laughter, but at least he turned me loose to concentrate on his sons.

Amazingly, Lloyd had heard. He looked right at me, smiled and waved, a gesture that cost him the race. The time Lloyd had taken to acknowledge me was all Boyd needed to reach the bell rope. As the tones of the ringing spread in waves over us, I noticed one of the ranch hands known as Old Claude standing in the archway below the bell. His head was cocked as though he were listening carefully, and I thought he must be hard of hearing.

As we were packing to leave the next day, someone brought news that Old Claude was dead. Then in the car on the way home, Mother mentioned that every couple of years someone seemed to die around the time of the twins' birthday. Father joked grimly that maybe our visits brought bad luck.

Their words set me thinking, and I tried to recall others who had died. I didn't know of anyone else, but my uncle's ranch was large and many people worked for him. Also, when I was younger, the adults might have been less likely to talk about death in front of me.

The following August, Boyd again won the race to the bell tower. As the bell began to ring, I looked down the tower to where Lloyd clung with a grin and a shrug of defeat. At the base of the tower, in the centre of the arch, stood McLeod, a border collie. A memory stirred of the year before and a wave of uneasiness passed over me, but the feeling passed before the memory could come into focus.

At breakfast the next morning, Lloyd told me one of the dogs had died the night before.

"McLeod?" I asked instantly.

"Yes," he said, surprised. "How did you know?"

As soon as he mentioned death, I had remembered Old Claude. The last time I had seen him or the dog, each had been standing in the same place, just below the bell as Boyd rang it.

I looked up from my bowl of cereal and caught a thoughtful expression on Boyd's face.

"Hey, Hopeless, what are you staring at?" he asked, more from the habit of rudeness than from malice.

"Cut it out, Boyd," his brother said, but Lloyd's response was habit too. His mind wasn't really on me either.

The next year Lloyd won the race, giving support to my belief that he could win all the time if he wanted to. But that wasn't how Boyd saw it.

"You were lucky. My hands slipped." He had half a dozen excuses.

"I just needed the wish this year," Lloyd said.

"Wish?" I asked.

"Didn't you know?" Aunt Rosina asked. "The bell-ringer always gets a wish granted. It's an old tradition."

The next year Boyd won again. An elderly woman, one of the kitchen workers, died on the evening of the party. I hadn't watched the climb to the bell tower, and I bit my tongue every time I found myself about to ask where she was standing when the bell rang.

You don't know, I told myself. But I couldn't stop myself from watching Boyd. Did he know? That was the question I wanted to ask.

After that birthday my family moved, and we were no longer able to travel to Aunt Rosina's and Uncle Jordan's every summer. I often thought about those colourful birthdays, but over the next two years the bell in the archway began to seem like a faded memory. The pattern I thought I had seen and the question of whether Boyd knew and was a deliberate murderer seemed to recede. I started to think of all that as a silly childhood fantasy. How can you kill by making a wish and ringing a bell?

I was fifteen when my family went back to visit our relatives during summer vacation, a vacation that just happened to include the date of the twins' birth. Boyd and Lloyd were celebrating their eighteenth birthday.

"Surely they're too big for the race this year," my

mother said.

"Too big for wishes? Never!" Uncle Jordan replied. "Besides, I want to see who's my stronger boy this year." He gave his shout of laughter and clapped his sons on their shoulders.

I was no longer frightened of him, at least not the way I'd been at seven or eight. But I did not like my uncle. It wasn't just his loudness; it was his ferocious competitiveness. Even as he challenged his sons, I could see Boyd dart an unfriendly look at his brother.

The next day was as noisy and colourful as those magnificent birthdays always were. I still liked the food and filled my plate, jealously guarding it for old times' sake. I went back for more enchiladas, chiles rellenos, guacamole and tomato salad, and finally, flan, chosen from a table crowded with desserts.

The games had changed over the years. So that afternoon I watched a dozen or more young men play ball. Then I joined them for horseback riding.

I loved horses and I loved the idea of riding, but I'd never had much experience. Uncle Jordan, who was assigning horses to us looked at me sceptically.

"I don't think ..." he began, pulling his lower lip as he studied my slight build.

"Give her Mariposa," Lloyd told his father.

"No!" his father said, falling back as though staggered by the thought. "A thoroughbred like that for a little turnip to ride? She'll never hold her."

I could see he was making fun of me and understood

from his tone that Mariposa was gentle.

She also turned out to be fat and slow, but my ride was only part reality; the other part was supplied by my own imagination. In my mind, my little grey Mariposa was a wild black stallion that only I could ride. I could not keep up with the others, all of whom were more experienced riders than I. So I missed some of the afternoon's excitement.

I never got the whole story of it, but I learned enough to know that Boyd had insisted on a contest and that Lloyd had beaten him.

As we rode back, Boyd galloped past me. A glimpse of his face made me feel cold in spite of the warmth of the late afternoon. The old, buried fears stirred in me.

Just as we all began to return from the stables, the birthday cake, topped by sparklers, was brought out. With more than fifty guests to be served, cutting the cake took us through the first shadows of evening.

Maybe, I thought, *they've waited too late for the bell ringing this year.* I couldn't believe my old suspicions, but I couldn't entirely forget them either. I was walking slowly, eating my cake as I thought about all those other years. Passing beside a group seated under a tree, I heard someone saying, "So terrible – the accident that killed Pepe just this time last year."

I froze in my tracks and stood listening.

"I remember he was struck by farm machinery. I thought it happened during the harvest."

"No, it was exactly a year ago. I know when I heard

the news I thought how I had seen him the evening
before, standing under the bell in the archway."

It has to be stopped, I thought. With the crowds of
people that were brought in each year for the festival,
the odds were great that someone would be under the
arch that held the bell when everyone's attention was
focused on the bell ringing. As I pondered what I had
heard, I was moving steadily in the direction of the
tower. All my doubts were gone; I felt the same horror I
had felt in years before.

Just then Uncle Jordan boomed out, "Time for the
bell ringing."

"Let's start the race from here," Boyd said, wiping his
mouth with the back of his hand. I could see both my
cousins, though I was now nearer to the tower than
they were.

The two of them began to run as soon as Boyd spoke,
and I could see that the competition had become even
more fierce in the last few years. They had passed me
and were very nearly at the base of the tower when
Lloyd fell. I was not sure how he had done it, but I had
the clear impression that Boyd had engineered the fall.
Once again the warm desert air was dispelled by an icy
cold, just as it had been by Boyd's murderous look
earlier. Pushing through the crowd, I began moving to
the bell tower, openly running as soon as I found a
clear path.

Even as I ran, I saw Boyd grip the rough stone of the
wall and begin to climb, moving more smoothly and

faster than on those long-ago birthdays.

Does he have some awful power? I wondered. *He can't,*
I answered myself. *He must have!* I argued as I ran. As
Boyd reached the top, Lloyd was still shaking himself off,
standing there beside the bell tower. Boyd reached out;
his hand touched the bell rope. But he didn't pull it. He
leaned forwards, straining to see his brother.

Lloyd was on the far side from his appointed climbing
wall. To reach it he'd have to pass beneath the arch. I
was close enough to touch the arch now myself and with
every step I willed Lloyd to stop. Boyd had won; there
was no need to go on. Still Boyd waited, as though to
give his brother a chance.

Under the darkening blue sky, the adobe archway
stood like a black shadow.

"Ring it," someone yelled. "Ring it! Ring it!" sounded
from all sides. I began to shout too. Still the bell
was silent.

"Don't wait for him!" Uncle Jordan called out to his
son on the tower. "Don't wait. You've won."

But he **was** waiting for something. Clinging to the side
of the tower, Boyd leaned far out. He had coiled the bell
rope around his shoulders, claiming the bell for his own.
Since he wasn't waiting to give Lloyd a chance, what was
he doing?

As though in slow motion, I saw Lloyd reach the
archway. A few more steps and he'd be directly
underneath the bell. That was what Boyd was
waiting for.

I glanced back up at Boyd and jumped in surprise as his eyes met mine.

As clearly as though he'd spoken, I could hear him saying, *So you know too, little Hopeless.*

Propelled forwards by his unspoken words or the hatred behind them, I sprang into motion. In a running tackle worthy of any of the boys I'd watched that afternoon, I landed on my cousin Lloyd, throwing both of us to the ground beyond the archway where we hit with a thud that knocked the wind out of me.

As we struggled to disentangle ourselves, I heard moans and cries from the spectators. At first I thought they were for us, Lloyd and me sprawled on the ground, but a noise like the roar of a wounded elephant drowned the other cries.

As my uncle's face swam into my dazed vision, I knew something more than our fall was wrong. Lloyd saw his brother before I did and tried to block my view, but Boyd, hanging from the end of the bell rope, swung into sight. He had leaned too far, trying to see what was happening to Lloyd and me; and that rope around his shoulders had been a mistake. In trying so hard to be certain of Lloyd's position, he had slipped and fallen.

All around me I heard shrieks of grief from the family and guests. Beside me, Lloyd began to shake with dry sobs. I thought I should feel sorry too, but all I could feel was relief that Boyd would not make any more birthday wishes.

Those
who'll
play
with
cats
must
expect
to
be
scratched.

CERVANTES

THE
CREATURE
IN
THE
DOORWAY

T he tail was the part of the creature Jeff Pardee saw first, though he didn't know then that it was a tail. In his seat by the window, Jeff was the width of the room away from the classroom door, but he could see the doorway perfectly well. And he could see the black velvet rope that lay just inside the door. As he watched, it rose in a lazy, looping motion and thrashed down against the floor. No, not a rope, something living.

He had mistaken it for a rope, but not for a moment could it be mistaken for a snake. No snake could rise so completely or fall with that graceful power. What he was seeing was a cat's tail, only twenty times bigger than the tail of any house cat. Staring hard at the shadows in the partially opened door, Jeff thought he could see the curve of a dark haunch. He watched, mesmerized by the motions – the flicks and lashes of the tail – until biology class was almost over. A shuffling of paper around him

drew his attention to the other students. None of them
seemed to have noticed the creature in the doorway.
When their books were stacked, a few of those most
eager to be out of class glanced towards the corridor, but
nobody screamed or pointed or even commented.

Jeff kept quiet too.

In English and geometry classes, the teachers kept the
doors closed, so Jeff had no chance to watch the corridor
for another glimpse of the dark creature. By noon he
began to think he had been dreaming in biology. But
during the first class after lunch, the creature came back.

Miss Sorrel always left the door ajar in the French
room – "*pour le vent de travers,* or to get a cross-current,"
she would explain.

In this class Jeff sat closer to the door and he saw the
big black creature come and first drop to its haunches
and then stretch out just outside the door with its tail
trailing into the French room.

A panther, Jeff thought. What other cat could be so
large? *A black panther.* He watched it with hungry
interest through the rest of the class period.

On the following day Jeff kept an eye on the door all
through biology class, but the panther did not come.
Between classes he tried to look up and down the
corridors, but the crowds of kids moving between
classrooms and lockers blocked his view. By the time
he reached his own locker and switched books, he was
almost late for class. At the door of the geometry room,
he paused as the bell rang. Glancing once more up and

then down the corridor, he spied the panther walking
away from him. The animal seemed to sense Jeff's gaze.
The huge cat's head swung slowly around on its well-
muscled neck. The panther's eyes did not meet Jeff's, but
the great creature held his head in profile as though
acknowledging an admirer.

In the library that afternoon, Jeff picked up volume
"P" of the encyclopedia.

"Whatcha lookin' up?" asked Richard, who shared a
table with him.

"Nothin'." Jeff shrugged. And he soon found out he
had spoken more truly than he had intended.

"Panther," he read, "is a name given to the leopard."
He took the volume back and exchanged it for the
"L" volume.

Sliding back into his chair and flipping the pages
he found the entry for "Leopard". *Ah, this is more like it,*
he thought.

"Leopards are the third largest cats in the world. Only
lions and tigers are larger."

Jeff stopped and thought. The only time he had seen
the full length of the leopard had been in the hallway,
and then he had seen him from behind so it was hard
to judge size. Still, this black panther seemed bigger
than anything he had ever seen in a zoo – lion, tiger,
or whatever.

"An average leopard is about 60 centimetres high at
the shoulder and over two metres long," he read. "The
largest may be nearly three metres long. A male may

weigh between 45 and 75 kilograms, the female 25 kilograms. The black leopard is so dark the spots are almost impossible to see; the whole animal looks black.

"Leopards are climbers and spend part of each day in trees. They are meat-eaters, though they rarely attack humans. Incredibly strong, leopards have been known to drag 70 kilogram carcasses to branches six metres above the ground."

Jeff silently formed the word "wow" and closed the book.

At home that evening he looked up "Leopard" in a big book called *Animals of the World*. The illustration showed a leopard pouncing on a deer. "Leopards hunt monkeys, sheep, jackals, goats, and antelopes," Jeff read. This book too said that leopards don't usually attack people.

"But once an individual leopard discovers people are easy prey, he becomes more dangerous than a tiger."

Prey? Jeff pondered, as he closed the book. *I wonder if I'm prey to my leopard. Is he stalking me?*

Jeff wasn't prepared for biology class, but he wasn't worried. The odds of being called on in a class of thirty-eight people were very small. In fact, he imagined he could slip almost unnoticed right through his high school years if he really tried. He sat in class wishing he could draw cartoons as Richard did to pass the time. Then, ten minutes before the bell, Mr Berrens walked over and opened the door.

The panther must have been leaning against it because he sprawled into the room as the door moved back. With his hand on the door and his eyes still on his book, Mr Berrens stepped away.

Jeff held his breath, afraid to move, frightened that everyone around him would see the panther. No one did. Class went on just as before.

That afternoon Jeff was watching the panther through the open door of the French room. The class was translating a story about a girl who came home to find her friends making a mess of her room, playing her records, and even disturbing her goldfish.

"*Qui a insulté mon poisson rouge?* Who insulted my goldfish?" someone translated.

Jeff tried to focus his attention on the French book, but soon his eyes wandered to the shadowy form in the doorway. Miss Sorrel wouldn't like it; she'd drive it away. Jeff wondered how you tell someone in French that she had insulted your panther.

"Richard!" Miss Sorrel said sharply in the tone of a teacher calling a name the second time. Jeff turned to look at Richard, whose mind had clearly not been on French class. Perhaps Richard had also seen the panther. Jeff regarded him with interest.

"What was the question, Miss Sorrel?"

"Didn't you hear the question, Richard?"

"I'm sorry, Miss Sorrel. I was drawing a cartoon of insulting a goldfish."

The class laughed and Jeff turned away, feeling oddly relieved. Richard's distraction had had nothing to do with the panther. Jeff was beginning to think of the panther as his own.

He wasn't curious about why only he could see the leopard; he was just grateful. Whatever the leopard's business with him, it was private, just between the two of them.

For more than a week, Jeff watched the panther. Long classes, boring classes flew by unnoticed. His only thought was for the sight of the sleek black fur. Through open doors of classrooms he watched the creature. Sometimes in the halls between throngs of blue-jeaned legs, he would see the easy slouch of its movement.

He felt certain the panther was aware of him, but it never looked directly at him. *I'm always watching him, but if he sees me at all I don't know it.*

One day as Jeff stared at the flip-flop of the leopard's tail, Miss Sorrel called on him to translate the French lesson. Jeff looked at the open page in front of him. He knew he had the right page, but what had just been read? He searched frantically for his place and looked up bewildered. A movement at the door caught his eye and he saw the great cat stretch languidly, extending one leg with its huge hind paw into the classroom.

Heartened by the sight, Jeff looked again at the page and started to read: "*La forêt est verte et sombre. Ici le léopard habite.* The forest is green and dark. Here the leopard lives."

"*Très bien.* Very good, Jeff." Miss Sorrel praised him.

Jeff sighed, followed the translation for the rest of the page, and only then looked up to find his panther had gone.

"Major move in French class! You've got Miss Sorrel fooled," Richard told him later. "How about playing tennis after school?"

Jeff shook his head. "Maybe tomorrow."

Often after school, he lingered in the halls hoping for a last sight of his panther.

It's as much a case of my stalking him as of his stalking me, Jeff told himself on the way home. "Friend or foe?" he chanted to himself, climbing the stairs to his room. "Friend or foe? That's what I would like to know."

Laughing at himself, he threw his book bag on to the bed and raised the shade of his window.

He almost stumbled backwards. The usually bare limbs of the tree by the window weren't bare any longer. Stretched full length, arrogant and imperturbable, the leopard lay on a branch just beyond the glass.

As Jeff stared open-mouthed, the bold head lifted and the great yellow eyes looked straight into his. He heard his mother calling. Held by the gaze, he stayed where he was. Looking into the creature's eyes for the first time, he felt certain that he was chosen rather than chased. The yellow eyes slowly closed and opened, and Jeff was released from their spell. His question answered, he mouthed "thanks" towards the beast and hurried to find his mother.

Deep in the night, groggy with sleep and dreams, Jeff was disturbed by a rattling at his window. He turned one ear into the pillow and tried to ignore the noise, but it just grew more insistent. Finally he got out of his tousled bed and made his way to the window. Gripping the ledge, he studied the tree by the light of the moon. The huge cat was back, and on a branch opposite him was a second, slightly smaller cat, just as dark and imposing as Jeff's cat.

"What?" Jeff asked, befuddled by the sight. "What is it you want?"

The branch on which the larger cat lay rocked and tapped at the window again.

Hastily Jeff opened the window, wrestled with the shutter for a moment, and then pulled it free.

"Come in," he invited, stepping aside. He eased himself back into the shadows and waited.

For a long time nothing happened. Then he saw the forepaws of the smaller cat land on the window sill, while the hind legs still rested on the tree. After another long wait, she slid through the window. (This one, Jeff decided, had to be "she", the mate of his panther.) Moments passed and Jeff held his breath as long as he could. At length the cat chose to settle herself under Jeff's bed. Still Jeff waited.

When it became obvious that the male would not follow her into the room, Jeff replaced the screen and exchanged another long look with the huge creature outside before closing the window.

Before morning, the panther under Jeff's bed gave birth to four cubs. Jeff moved most of his bedding on to the floor to provide a nest for the mother and her young.

Leaving for school the next day, he posted his DO NOT DISTURB sign on the door of his room – not that his mother ever entered anyway.

"It smells," she would say, "and the whole mess is so depressing."

If his mother wanted to complain this morning, Jeff had to admit that she would have a reason.

It does smell odd, he thought. But he'd have to disagree about the depressing part. His room had never been more interesting or more exciting.

From the corner of his eye he watched the black panther all day at school. In the evening, sitting at a respectful distance, he watched the mother and her cubs. When the male climbed the tree with the carcass of his prey, Jeff opened the window so that the two leopards could share their meal.

After a few days Jeff fell into the habit of sitting up late watching the cubs and then stretching out to sleep on the floor in front of his door.

After two months of sharing his bedroom with the cats, Jeff came home one day to find them gone. He searched the house first, then his garden, and finally he climbed the tree. Nothing. Not a sign of the panthers anywhere.

Too depressed to clean his room or reclaim his bed, he once again slept on the floor.

"You look like something the cat dragged in," his mother told him at breakfast the next morning. "Comb your hair and pull yourself together."

All day he watched for the panther at school but didn't catch sight of him. At night he tried to ignore the emptiness of his room. By the end of the week, he decided the panther and his family were gone for good.

In the following week Jeff had to write an essay about the poem "Tyger, Tyger," for English class. He read that William Blake was a poet who had the "courage to risk obscurity". Jeff didn't think that took courage; all poems were pretty obscure. And besides, "Tyger, Tyger" seemed clearer to him than most poems.

> Tyger! Tyger! burning bright
> In the forests of the night,
> What immortal hand or eye
> Could frame thy fearful symmetry?

Like the poet, Jeff had spent time wondering about the origin of a big, deadly cat. He wrote about Blake's poem, thought about his panther, and earned a B+ on his essay.

From his biology textbook, he learned that the leopard's scientific name is *felis pardus*. Even his schoolwork seemed designed to keep his mind on his panthers.

More out of habit than hope, he continued to look for his cats. Once he thought he saw the big male turning a corner in the hall but concluded he had just seen a shadow when he chased it and found nothing.

One Friday afternoon going home on the bus, he was

staring dully out of the window when he became aware of a blacker area of the bus's shadow. Instantly after, he sat up, peered down beside the bus and saw the panther, sleek and long-legged, moving fluidly beside them, keeping pace with the bus.

Concentrating all his attention on the big cat, Jeff kept him in sight until the bus stopped at his own corner. He climbed off, still keeping an eye on the panther. The huge creature halted in the shadow until the bus pulled away and then he moved with big-footed grace on to the path beside Jeff.

Just at the point where Jeff would have left the walkway to go into his house, the leopard turned aside in the opposite direction. Afraid to let it out of his sight, Jeff followed. At first at a casual walk and then, matching strides, speeding up to an easy run, the two moved into the trees, past a tumbled-down barbed-wire fence, to the edge of a creek.

The panther stopped and looked directly at Jeff. Ahead of them the mother and cubs were dark spots amid splashes of sun through the trees. Cautiously, Jeff edged towards them, leaving his book bag behind under a tree.

One – two – three. One cub was missing. Now both adults were staring at him.

"Where's the other one?" he asked softly and began to look around.

Angry kitten sounds drew him to a patch of bramble. The cub was clearly visible under a tent of prickly vines.

Why doesn't he crawl out? Jeff wondered.

The cat looked trapped but the thorns alone shouldn't have been enough to stop him. Jeff studied the situation, the parents watching as he tried to understand the cub's plight.

Growling and meowing, the cub roamed about his enclosure. A sudden movement tumbled him over, and then Jeff saw the problem: one paw was caught fast, tangled in a strand of wire.

Pushing his hands gingerly through the brambles, Jeff reached the cub. He rubbed its head, scratched its ears to reassure it, and then felt along the hind leg until he touched the wire. The wire couldn't be broken. He'd have to untwist it. Taking the small cat in one hand and manoeuvring through the briars, he grasped the wire with the fingers of his right hand.

Trickles of blood were running down his arms where he had torn them on the thorns. Manipulating the wire, he tried to free the cat. Once it cried out in pain, and Jeff quickly reversed the direction he was turning the wire. After a while, he slid the cub and his own bloodied hands out of the thorny enclosure.

Pushing past Jeff, the mother claimed her fourth cub and began washing it, the force of her tongue rolling it over on the leaves.

For long moments Jeff watched, tolerantly ignored by the cats. Then, regretfully, he gathered up his book bag and left the cat family to its woodland privacy.

On Saturday morning, Jeff lay in bed wondering what

had awakened him at five o'clock. He rolled on his side and stared at a corner of his rug, frayed by the cats' chewing. Just as he began to debate the possibility of seeking them out again, he heard the familiar scratching at the window.

He sprang out of bed in a single motion, threw open the window, and thrust aside the shutter. They were back – the male, the female, and all four cubs. The mother and the cubs came through the window first. And this time, the big male followed them in.

Of course there won't be room for me any more, Jeff decided as they settled themselves around his room. *But who needs a bedroom?* He laughed out loud.

To most of the leopard family, he soon became no more than a shadowy form that occasionally appeared in their doorway, watching as they pursued their cat lives in the lair of his bedroom.

Before long, however, one small cub with a bandaged hind paw, began to follow Jeff out of the room, to lie curling around his feet at the supper table, chewing at his shoes, and purring when Jeff slipped him table scraps.

380790006300905